Whispers of the Willowbrook Estate's Spectral Circus

Mapping the Uncharted Landscapes of Dreams and Subconscious Mind with the Aid of Cosmological Cartography and Botanical Necromancy

Holden Riversong

Table of Contents

Table of Contents

1 Prologue: Willowbrook's Enigma

The air hung heavy, thick with the scent of decaying leaves and damp earth. A peculiar stillness blanketed Willowbrook Estate, broken only by the rustling of wind-stirred willows that lined the long, neglected driveway. Their branches, skeletal fingers against the twilight sky, seemed to beckon towards the imposing manor. Its darkened windows stared back, vacant eyes reflecting the deepening gloom, hinting at secrets hidden within their depths. An almost imperceptible hum vibrated through the very ground, a low, resonant thrumming like a heartbeat from the earth itself. It pulsed with a strange, otherworldly energy, a preternatural resonance that hinted at the estate's unusual history. This was a place where the veil between worlds felt thin, where whispers of the past mingled with the present, creating an atmosphere ripe with spectral unease.

Willowbrook Estate had always been a place of whispers. Locals told tales of strange occurrences, of ghostly figures flitting through the overgrown gardens and eerie music drifting from the dilapidated ballroom. Children dared each other to venture near its wrought-iron gates, only to scurry away, their imaginations fueled by half-glimpsed shadows and the chilling sense of being watched. The stories varied, morphing over time like the twisting willows themselves, but one constant remained: Willowbrook was a place touched by something beyond the ordinary. Something that defied explanation. Something that whispered of a spectral circus. This circus, unseen by most, held an ephemeral presence, a phantasmagoria of sights and sounds that seemed to bleed from the very fabric of the estate itself. The history of Willowbrook was shrouded in obscurity, a tapestry woven with half-truths and local legends. Records spoke of a wealthy family, the Vandergeltens, who had built the estate in the late 19th century. They were known for their lavish parties, their eccentric tastes, and their fascination with the esoteric. Whispers hinted at séances held in the grand library, of attempts to contact the spirit world, and of a growing obsession with dreams and the subconscious. Then, tragedy struck. A series of unexplained deaths and disappearances plagued the family, casting a pall over Willowbrook and ultimately leading to its abandonment. The estate fell into disrepair, reclaimed by nature, becoming a silent testament to a forgotten past. But the past, it seemed, was far from silent. It resonated in the rustling willows, echoed in the empty halls, and played out in the spectral circus that continued its silent performance.

This spectral circus was more than just a haunting. It was a reflection, a distorted mirror image of the subconscious desires, fears, and forgotten memories that clung to Willowbrook like cobwebs. The ghostly performers were not merely apparitions; they were projections, fragments of shattered psyches given form by the estate's peculiar energies. They danced and cavorted in a silent pantomime, their movements both mesmerizing and unsettling, their spectral forms shimmering in and out of existence like flickering candle flames. The spectral big top, an ephemeral structure that appeared and disappeared with unsettling randomness, served as the stage for this otherworldly performance. Its tattered canvas billowed in an unseen breeze, casting long, distorted shadows across the overgrown lawns.

To understand the spectral circus, one had to understand the landscape of dreams. The subconscious mind, a vast and uncharted territory, held the key to unlocking Willowbrook's enigmas. It was a realm of symbols and metaphors, a world where the laws of logic held no sway. This was the realm where the spectral circus took root, where its phantasmagorical performances played out nightly for an audience of none. To navigate this realm, one needed a map, a guide to the labyrinthine pathways of the subconscious. Cosmological cartography, an ancient practice of mapping the celestial sphere and its perceived influence on the human mind, provided a starting point. By understanding the language of stars, the movements of planets, and the cycles of the cosmos, one could begin to chart the hidden currents of the subconscious. This was not mere astrology; it was a deeper exploration of the interconnectedness between the macrocosm and the microcosm, a journey into the very fabric of existence.

But the cosmos was not the only source of guidance. The earth itself held secrets, whispers of forgotten knowledge hidden within the decaying flora of Willowbrook's neglected gardens. Botanical necromancy, a practice steeped in both folklore and occult tradition, offered a different path to understanding the spectral circus. By communing with the spirits of dead plants, by tapping into the residual energies of Willowbrook's overgrown vegetation, one could glean insights into the past, unravel the mysteries of the estate, and perhaps even begin to communicate with the performers of the spectral circus.

Willowbrook Estate, with its spectral circus and whispers in the willows, was more than just a haunted house. It was a doorway, a threshold between worlds, a place where the boundaries of reality blurred and the secrets of the subconscious danced in the shadows. It was an enigma waiting to be solved, a mystery that beckoned to those brave enough to explore its depths. It was a call to delve into the uncharted landscapes of dreams, to map the hidden territories of the mind, and to uncover the truth behind the spectral circus that held Willowbrook captive. It was a journey into the unknown, a descent into the depths of the human psyche, where the answers, if they existed at all, were as elusive and ephemeral as the spectral performers themselves.

1.1   Whispers in the Willows

The air hung heavy with the scent of decaying leaves and damp earth. A spectral mist clung to the gnarled branches of the willow trees that lined the drive, their weeping forms casting long, skeletal shadows across the overgrown path. Here, at the edge of the Willowbrook Estate, the whispers began. Not audible whispers, precisely, but a subtle unsettling of the air, a prickling sensation at the back of the neck, an almost imperceptible shift in the quality of light. This was the threshold, the liminal space between the mundane and the spectral, where the veil between worlds thinned to the point of translucence. The willows themselves seemed to be conduits, their roots sunk deep into the earth, their branches reaching towards the heavens, drawing power from both realms. They swayed gently in the breeze, their leaves rustling like hushed secrets, beckoning you deeper into the estate's embrace.

Willowbrook had always been a place of mystery, its history woven from equal parts grandeur and tragedy. Generations of families had lived and died within its walls, their joys and sorrows imprinted upon the very fabric of the estate. These echoes of the past, the residue of human emotion, clung to the air like cobwebs, catching the light in peculiar ways, manifesting as fleeting glimpses of movement in the periphery. It was a place where the mundane bled into the magical, where the spectral circus held its nightly performances, beckoning those brave or foolish enough to seek its mysteries. The whispers grew stronger as you approached the main house, a looming Victorian edifice with boarded-up windows and a crumbling facade. The paint peeled away like sunburnt skin, revealing the bare wood beneath, scarred and weathered by time and neglect. The air grew colder, a chill that seeped into your bones, defying the mild autumn afternoon. A strange disquiet settled in your stomach, a feeling of being watched, of being drawn into something beyond your comprehension.

Observe the architecture closely. Note the intricate carvings adorning the eaves, the gargoyles perched atop the roofline, their grotesque features frozen in perpetual sneers. These details, once symbols of wealth and status, now seemed ominous, imbued with a sinister energy. They whispered tales of forgotten rituals, of arcane practices performed under the cloak of darkness, of a family's desperate attempts to commune with the other side. The whispers led you toward the overgrown gardens, a labyrinth of tangled vines and decaying statues, where the spectral circus pitched its ethereal tent. The air thrummed with an unseen energy, a palpable sense of anticipation. Faint music drifted through the air, a melancholic melody played on a phantom calliope, its notes tinged with both joy and sorrow. The scent of popcorn and cotton candy mingled with the earthy aroma of decaying vegetation, creating a bizarre olfactory cocktail that assaulted the senses.

Focus on the interplay of light and shadow within the garden. Notice how the moonlight filtered through the leaves, creating an otherworldly glow, illuminating the spectral performers as they took their places. The clowns, with their painted smiles and hollow eyes, stumbled through their routines, their laughter echoing eerily through the night. The trapeze artists soared through the air, their movements graceful and fluid, defying gravity with effortless ease. The strongman, his muscles bulging, lifted impossible weights, his grunts of exertion punctuated by the crack of a spectral whip. The ringmaster, a shadowy figure in a top hat and tails, orchestrated the entire spectacle, his voice a hypnotic whisper that resonated deep within your soul.

Each performance was a reflection of the subconscious mind, a manifestation of the hopes, fears, and desires that lurked beneath the surface of conscious thought. The clowns represented the hidden sadness, the pain masked by forced smiles. The trapeze artists symbolized the yearning for freedom, the desire to escape the constraints of the physical world. The strongman embodied the struggle for control, the battle against inner demons. And the ringmaster, the enigmatic conductor of this spectral orchestra, represented the elusive self, the hidden architect of our dreams and nightmares. To understand the whispers, one must delve into the symbolic language of the circus, unraveling the complex tapestry of meaning woven into each performance. This requires a willingness to confront the shadows of the subconscious, to explore the darker corners of the mind, to embrace the duality of laughter and tears, of joy and sorrow.

This exploration, however, was not without its dangers. The spectral circus was a seductive mistress, its allure both captivating and terrifying. It offered glimpses into the hidden depths of the self, but it also threatened to consume those who dared to venture too deep. To navigate this treacherous landscape, one needed a map, a guide to the uncharted realms of the subconscious. This map could be found in the language of the stars, in the whispers of dead flora, in the ancient practice of botanical necromancy. By deciphering the celestial charts, by communing with the spirits of deceased plants, one could gain insight into the mysteries of the spectral circus and unlock the secrets of Willowbrook Estate. This journey, however, was not for the faint of heart. It demanded courage, curiosity, and a willingness to embrace the unknown. It required a suspension of disbelief, a willingness to accept the impossible as possible, to see the magic that shimmered just beneath the surface of the mundane world. The whispers beckoned, promising enlightenment and understanding, but also warning of the perils that awaited those who dared to heed their call. The choice, as always, was yours. Would you venture into the spectral big top and confront the shadows of your subconscious? Or would you turn away, content to remain in the mundane world, forever ignorant of the mysteries that lay hidden just beyond the veil?

1.2   The Spectral Big Top

The air crackled with an unseen energy. Not a tangible electricity, but a psychic vibration, a shimmering tremor in the very fabric of Willowbrook. Here, within the decaying grandeur of the estate, the veil between worlds thinned, allowing glimpses into the spectral realm. Specifically, the decaying remnants of a once-grand circus tent materialized and dematerialized within the overgrown gardens, its tattered canvas flapping like a ghostly sigh. This was the Spectral Big Top, a phantasmagorical spectacle, an echo of a forgotten entertainment, now twisted into a bizarre reflection of the subconscious mind. The scent of sawdust and stale popcorn hung heavy in the air, a phantom aroma that tickled the nostrils, hinting at a reality just beyond our grasp. Faint strains of a distorted calliope wheezed on the wind, a melancholic melody hinting at joys and sorrows long past.

This ethereal circus, more dream than reality, served as a gateway. A gateway to the uncharted landscapes of the subconscious. It was a swirling vortex of vibrant, distorted imagery: clowns with painted smiles that hid an unsettling emptiness, spectral trapeze artists defying gravity with impossible feats, and phantom strongmen bending bars of moonlight. The tent itself pulsed with an otherworldly luminescence, its tattered flags emblazoned with symbols that mirrored the constellations charted in ancient cosmological maps. These weren't just random apparitions. They were projections, manifestations of the deep-seated desires, fears, and unresolved conflicts that resided within the shadowed recesses of the human mind. Each contorted figure, each eerie act, whispered a story. A story of forgotten memories, repressed emotions, and the eternal struggle between the conscious and subconscious.

Observe the tightrope walker. He teeters precariously across a shimmering thread of moonlight, balancing a stack of crumbling hourglasses. This symbolizes the precarious balance of time, the constant pressure of deadlines and the fear of time slipping away. His every sway and stumble mirror our own anxieties about the fleeting nature of existence. Now, look closely at the clowns. Their painted grins are grotesquely exaggerated, their laughter a hollow, echoing sound. They represent the masks we wear in our waking lives, the forced cheerfulness that hides inner turmoil. Their silent tears, glimpsed in the flickering shadows, speak volumes about the pain concealed beneath the façade.

To truly understand the Spectral Big Top, one must first grasp the principles of cosmological cartography. This ancient practice, steeped in mysticism, views the cosmos as a mirror of the human psyche. Just as the stars form constellations, so too do our thoughts and emotions coalesce into patterns within the subconscious. By studying the movements of celestial bodies, we can gain insight into the hidden currents that shape our dreams and influence our waking lives. The constellations etched upon the spectral tent flags are not mere decorations. They are a coded language, a celestial script that reveals the intricate connections between the macrocosm and the microcosm. Each symbol corresponds to a specific archetype, a universal pattern of human experience. Deciphering these symbols unlocks a deeper understanding of the spectral circus and its profound implications. Further exploration requires venturing into the realm of botanical necromancy. This is not a practice for the faint of heart. It involves communing with the spirits of deceased plants, harnessing their residual energies to amplify our perception of the spectral realm. Specifically, the withered roses scattered around the base of the spectral tent hold a key. These aren't ordinary roses. They are imbued with the psychic residue of forgotten emotions, the echoes of laughter and tears shed within the grounds of Willowbrook. By carefully preparing a tincture from their petals, and reciting the incantations found within the Green Grimoire, we can attune ourselves to the subtle vibrations emanating from the Spectral Big Top. This will enhance our ability to perceive and interpret the symbolic language of the spectral circus.

The swirling mists that shroud the big top are not just visual effects. They are a psychic veil, a barrier between the conscious and subconscious. To penetrate this veil, we must adopt a specific mindset, a state of receptive awareness that allows us to bypass the filters of the rational mind. Close your eyes, breathe deeply, and focus your attention on the faint calliope music. Let the melancholic melody wash over you, carrying you deeper into the ethereal realm. As you surrender to the rhythm, you will find yourself drawn closer to the heart of the Spectral Big Top, where the secrets of the subconscious await.

This is where the true work begins. By combining the insights gained through cosmological cartography and botanical necromancy, we can begin to unravel the intricate tapestry of the subconscious mind. The Spectral Big Top is not just a spectacle to be observed. It is a living map, a dynamic representation of our inner world. Each encounter with the spectral circus offers a unique opportunity for self-discovery, a chance to confront our deepest fears and unlock our hidden potential. The path may be challenging, but the rewards are immeasurable.

1.3 A Map of Dreams

Imagine the subconscious as a vast, uncharted territory. A wilderness of thoughts, memories, and emotions, tangled like overgrown vines in a forgotten garden. To navigate this terrain, we need a map, a guide to the hidden pathways and obscured landmarks of our inner world. This map isn't drawn with ink and parchment, but with the ephemeral stuff of dreams. It's a living document, constantly evolving, shifting with the tides of our experiences and the whispers of our deepest selves. The spectral circus of Willowbrook Estate serves as a tangible manifestation of this internal landscape, a bizarre and fantastical mirror reflecting the hidden contours of the subconscious.

Understanding the symbolism embedded within the circus is key to deciphering the map of your dreams. Every element, from the melancholic clowns to the gravity-defying trapeze artists, holds a specific meaning, a coded message from the depths of your being. Consider the ringmaster, a figure of authority and control. Does he represent your conscious mind, attempting to impose order on the chaotic swirl of the subconscious? Or perhaps he embodies an external force, societal expectations or ingrained beliefs, dictating the performance of your inner life. The trapeze artists, soaring through the air with effortless grace, might symbolize the aspirations and desires that lift you towards your potential. Their daring feats could represent the risks you must take to achieve your goals, the leaps of faith required to break free from the constraints of the familiar.

The spectral calliope's haunting melody weaving through the dream landscape represents the emotional undercurrents that shape your subconscious experience. Is the music joyful and uplifting, or tinged with melancholy and regret? The emotional tone of the music provides crucial clues about the underlying mood and message of your dreams. The clowns, with their painted smiles and silent tears, embody the duality of the human experience. They represent the masks we wear, the outward expressions that often conceal deeper, more complex emotions. Their silent tears speak to the unspoken sorrows and hidden vulnerabilities that reside within us all.

To effectively map your dreams, cultivate a practice of meticulous observation. Upon waking, immediately record every detail you can recall, no matter how trivial it may seem. Note the setting, the characters, the objects, the emotions evoked. Pay attention to recurring motifs and symbols, as these often hold significant personal meaning. As you accumulate a collection of dream records, begin to look for patterns and connections. Which symbols appear most frequently? What emotions tend to dominate your dream world? These observations provide valuable insights into the recurring themes and underlying dynamics of your subconscious.

Imagine the grounds of Willowbrook Estate itself as a metaphorical representation of your mind. The whispering willows, their branches swaying in the ethereal breeze, symbolize the subtle intuitions and fleeting thoughts that dance at the periphery of your awareness. The spectral big top, with its swirling lights and otherworldly atmosphere, represents the dream world itself, a place where the ordinary rules of reality dissolve and the subconscious takes center stage.

Think of cosmological cartography as a framework for understanding the interconnectedness of your inner and outer worlds. Just as the celestial bodies exert a gravitational pull on the physical world, so too do the archetypes and universal symbols influence the landscape of the subconscious. By studying the language of the stars, you gain a deeper understanding of the symbolic language of your dreams. Botanical necromancy, in this context, represents the practice of tapping into the wisdom of the natural world to gain insight into your own inner nature. The whispers of dead flora offer a connection to the ancestral knowledge and primal instincts that reside within your subconscious.

By combining the principles of cosmological cartography and botanical necromancy with the practice of dream mapping, you gain a powerful tool for self-discovery and personal transformation. This holistic approach allows you to navigate the uncharted landscapes of your dreams, uncover hidden truths about yourself, and ultimately, rewrite the narrative of your own life. The spectral circus of Willowbrook Estate becomes not a place of fear and confusion, but a vibrant classroom, a mystical guide leading you on a journey of self-exploration and profound understanding. It becomes a map, not just of dreams, but of the very essence of your being.

2 Cartography of the Cosmos

The human mind, a universe unto itself, mirrors the vast expanse of the cosmos. Ancient cultures recognized this inherent connection, weaving intricate tapestries of myth and meaning between the celestial tapestry and the inner world. Consider the Egyptians, who saw the Nile's yearly inundation mirroring the celestial journey of the sun god Ra, believing their inner lives were intimately tied to the cosmic rhythm. This chapter unveils the powerful cartography that links the external cosmos and the internal landscape of dreams, opening pathways to navigate the subconscious terrain of Willowbrook Estate. Think of this as drawing your own personal star chart, but instead of plotting constellations, you are charting the unexplored territories of your inner world.

We begin by recognizing the symbolic resonance between celestial bodies and psychological archetypes. The radiant sun, for instance, often represents the conscious self, the driving force of our personality. The moon, veiled in mystery and cyclical change, embodies the ebb and flow of our emotions, the shadowy realm of the subconscious. The planets, each with its unique orbit and characteristics, mirror various aspects of our inner selves: Mercury's quick wit, Venus's allure, Mars's fiery drive. By studying these celestial correspondences, we can gain a deeper understanding of the forces at play within our own minds, uncovering hidden patterns and motivations that shape our dreams and influence the ethereal circus unfolding within Willowbrook. Imagine it like learning a new language – the language of the stars – where each celestial body whispers secrets about the human psyche.

This cosmic language offers a framework for understanding the astral plane, the ethereal realm often accessed through dreams and altered states of consciousness. Consider the astral plane as an overlay of the physical world, a vibrant tapestry woven from thought and emotion. By attuning ourselves to the celestial rhythms, we can learn to navigate this subtle dimension, much like a sailor uses the stars to chart a course across the ocean. This navigation isn't about physical travel; it's about traversing the inner landscapes of Willowbrook, the subconscious realms where the spectral circus performs its enigmatic show. Imagine yourself drifting among constellations, each star a gateway to a different facet of your subconscious, each constellation a map to a unique dream realm.

This astral navigation requires a unique form of cartography, one that charts not physical locations, but the ethereal contours of the mind. Instead of longitude and latitude, we utilize symbols, archetypes, and intuitive understanding as our navigational tools. The "map" itself is not a static document, but a fluid, ever-shifting landscape, molded by our thoughts, emotions, and experiences. This map is intimately tied to the very fabric of Willowbrook, its spectral energies mirroring the subconscious currents flowing within us. Imagine tracing the paths of comets across your inner sky, their fiery trails illuminating forgotten memories, hidden desires, and the spectral figures that populate the dream circus.

Imagine the constellations themselves as gateways to different dream realms, each star a portal to a unique aspect of your subconscious. The constellations of the zodiac, for instance, offer a framework for understanding the cyclical patterns of our inner lives, their archetypal energies resonating with specific personality traits and emotional tendencies. By studying these celestial patterns and their corresponding psychological archetypes, we can learn to interpret the symbolic language of our dreams, deciphering the cryptic messages whispered by the spectral performers of Willowbrook's ethereal circus.

Furthermore, the movements of the planets through the zodiac offer another layer of insight into our inner landscapes. As each planet transits through a particular sign, its energy blends with the archetypal qualities of that sign, influencing our thoughts, emotions, and dreams. By understanding these planetary transits and their impact on our inner world, we can anticipate the shifting currents of the subconscious and navigate the ever-changing landscape of the dream circus with greater awareness and clarity. Consider how the full moon's amplified energy can illuminate the hidden corners of the mind, bringing subconscious content to the surface, while the new moon invites introspection and the planting of new seeds of intention within the dream realm. These celestial cycles provide a rhythm to our inner lives, much like the ebb and flow of the tides.

By learning to read the language of the stars, we equip ourselves with a powerful tool for navigating the subconscious realms and understanding the spectral whispers of Willowbrook Estate. We begin to see the dream circus not as a random assortment of phantasmagorical images, but as a reflection of our own inner world, a symbolic representation of our hopes, fears, and unresolved conflicts. Through this cosmic cartography, we can begin to chart a course toward greater self-awareness and unlock the hidden potential within the dreamscape, weaving our own narrative within the unending show of the subconscious mind. This journey is not merely about understanding the spectral circus, but about understanding ourselves. The cosmos within mirrors the cosmos without, and by mapping one, we gain insight into the other.

2.1   Celestial Charts & the Mind

The human mind, a universe unto itself, mirrors the vast expanse of the cosmos. Ancient cultures recognized this profound connection, weaving intricate tapestries of myth and meaning between the celestial bodies and the inner landscape of dreams. They understood that just as stars form constellations across the night sky, so too do thoughts, emotions, and memories cluster within the subconscious, creating patterns that shape our waking reality. This chapter explores the art of using celestial charts as a guide to navigate the uncharted territories of your own mind, a practice that lies at the heart of understanding the Spectral Circus of Willowbrook.

Imagine the night sky as a colossal mirror reflecting the hidden contours of your inner world. Each twinkling star represents a fragment of memory, a flicker of emotion, or a seed of potential. Just as astronomers chart the movements of celestial bodies, we can map the constellations of our subconscious, revealing hidden connections and illuminating the shadowy corners of our being. This is not mere metaphor. The ancients believed that specific stars and constellations held symbolic significance, resonating with particular aspects of the human psyche. By studying these celestial patterns, they sought to understand the forces that shaped human destiny and unlock the secrets of the inner world.

Consider, for instance, the constellation of Ursa Major, the Great Bear. In some traditions, this constellation represents strength, courage, and guardianship. By meditating on the image of Ursa Major, one might tap into these qualities within oneself, drawing upon their inner reserves of resilience and fortitude. Similarly, the constellation of Pisces, the Fishes, is often associated with intuition, empathy, and the realm of dreams. Focusing on Pisces might open pathways to deeper self-awareness and enhance one's ability to navigate the subtle currents of the subconscious. This isn't about literal influence from distant stars, but rather harnessing their symbolic power to illuminate the corresponding aspects of your inner world.

The practice of using celestial charts for self-exploration requires a shift in perspective. We must learn to see the night sky not just as a collection of distant objects, but as a symbolic representation of our own inner universe. This requires cultivating a sense of awe and wonder, an openness to the mysteries that lie beyond the grasp of our rational minds. Start by familiarizing yourself with the major constellations and their associated mythologies. Observe their positions in the sky throughout the year, noticing how their movements seem to echo the cyclical rhythms of your own life.

As you deepen your understanding of celestial cartography, begin to draw connections between the patterns in the sky and the patterns within your own mind. Which constellations resonate most strongly with you? What emotions or memories arise when you contemplate their symbolic meanings? Keep a dream journal and note any recurring symbols or themes. Do these connect to any particular constellations or astrological archetypes? This process of mapping your inner landscape can reveal hidden patterns and connections that might otherwise remain obscured. It can help you identify recurring themes, unresolved conflicts, and untapped potentials that reside within the depths of your subconscious.

This intimate connection between the cosmos and the subconscious is further amplified within the unique environment of Willowbrook Estate. The Spectral Circus, with its ethereal performers and dreamlike atmosphere, acts as a lens through which the whispers of the cosmos are magnified and made manifest. The celestial charts, then, become not just a map of your own mind, but a guide to navigating the bewildering and often unsettling landscape of the Spectral Circus.

Take, for example, the Phantom Calliope, whose haunting melodies weave through the estate grounds. Its music seems to shift and change in harmony with the celestial rhythms, its ethereal notes resonating with specific constellations. By understanding the symbolic language of the stars, we can begin to decipher the hidden messages embedded within the calliope's music, unlocking deeper layers of meaning within the spectral performance. The clowns' silent tears, too, reflect a celestial sorrow, mirroring the melancholic energy of certain stars.

The practice of mapping your inner landscape using celestial charts is not a quick fix or a simple formula. It requires patience, dedication, and a willingness to delve into the depths of your own being. It is a journey of self-discovery that can lead to profound insights and transformative experiences. By embracing the wisdom of the ancients and attuning ourselves to the whispers of the cosmos, we can begin to unravel the mysteries of the subconscious mind and navigate the spectral landscape of Willowbrook Estate with greater clarity and understanding. As you gaze upon the stars, remember that you are also looking inward, exploring the vast and uncharted territories of your own inner universe. The secrets of the Spectral Circus, and indeed the secrets of your own being, lie hidden within the constellations of your mind, waiting to be discovered.

2.2   Navigating the Astral Plane

The astral plane, a shimmering realm of thought and emotion, isn't a place you simply visit; it's a state of being you achieve. Think of it as an ocean of consciousness, vast and undulating, where the currents are formed by collective thoughts and emotions. Within this ocean, your own consciousness is a vessel, and navigating the astral plane requires understanding how to steer your ship. Preparation is key. Begin by cultivating a calm, focused mind. Meditation practices are invaluable here, allowing you to quiet the internal chatter and strengthen your mental focus, like honing the edge of a blade. Visualisation exercises are equally crucial, training your mind to create and maintain clear, vivid images. Imagine yourself standing on the deck of your ship, feeling the gentle rocking of the waves, the salt spray on your face. This practice will build your ability to consciously shape your astral experience.

Physical preparation also plays a significant role. Fasting or consuming light meals before attempting astral projection can lessen the pull of the physical body. Creating a peaceful, dimly lit environment, free from distractions, is essential. Incense or calming music can further enhance the atmosphere, creating a sanctuary for your journey. Think of it as preparing your vessel for a long voyage, ensuring it's well-stocked and seaworthy. A vital tool for astral navigation is the creation of an anchor point. This can be any physical object – a piece of jewelry, a stone, a familiar photograph – imbued with your intention and focus. Imagine this anchor point as a lighthouse, its beacon guiding you back to your physical body after your astral travels. Keep its image firmly in mind as you begin your journey, visualizing its details, its texture, its weight.

The actual process of astral projection can vary, but a common method involves deep relaxation and visualization. Lie comfortably, close your eyes, and systematically relax each muscle group, starting from your toes and working your way up to your head. As your body relaxes, your consciousness begins to loosen its grip on the physical realm. Imagine your astral body slowly rising from your physical form. Picture yourself floating above your bed, observing your sleeping form below. This separation, while initially disconcerting for some, is a crucial step in the process. Don't be alarmed. Remember your anchor point, the lighthouse in the distance.

Once separated, you'll find yourself in the vibrant landscape of the astral plane. It's a realm unbounded by physical laws, where thoughts manifest as tangible realities. You might encounter swirling colours, geometric patterns, or even encounter other beings, both benevolent and malevolent. Remember, your thoughts and emotions are your compass and rudder here. Fear can become a storm, tossing your astral vessel about, while confidence and clarity will steer you smoothly. Trust your intuition. It's the compass guiding you through these uncharted waters.

As you navigate this realm, maintaining focus is paramount. The astral plane is a fluid, ever-shifting landscape, susceptible to the influence of thoughts and emotions. Distractions can easily pull you off course, leading you into chaotic or undesirable areas. Focus on your intention, the purpose of your astral journey. Are you seeking answers to a particular question? Are you trying to connect with a specific energy? Holding this intention clearly in your mind, like a captain holding a steady course, will keep your journey focused and productive.

Remember the importance of grounding yourself upon your return. Reconnecting with your physical body should be a gradual, deliberate process. Visualize yourself descending back into your physical form, feeling the weight and solidity of your body returning. Once fully reintegrated, take a few moments to ground yourself. Eat something, drink some water, touch the earth. This helps to re-establish your connection to the physical world and integrate the insights you've gained on your astral journey.

Documenting your experiences is crucial. Keeping a journal dedicated to your astral travels allows you to track your progress, identify recurring patterns, and interpret the symbolism you encounter. Record your experiences in detail, including the emotions you felt, the images you saw, and any insights you received. Over time, this journal becomes a personalized map of your inner landscape, guiding you towards deeper understanding and self-discovery.

Exploring the astral plane is not a passive activity. It's an active engagement with your own consciousness, a journey of self-exploration and discovery. By cultivating focus, intention, and a healthy respect for the unseen forces at play, you can navigate this ethereal realm with confidence and glean profound insights into the mysteries of your own being. Each journey is unique, each experience a lesson, and each return a step further on the path to self-awareness. Remember the anchor point, the lighthouse guiding you home, and embark on your exploration with an open mind and a courageous spirit. The astral plane awaits.

2.3   The Language of Stars

The celestial tapestry woven across the night sky is more than a random scattering of light. It's a complex, symbolic language, whispering secrets to those who learn to listen. Each constellation, each individual star, vibrates with a unique frequency, a specific energy signature that resonates with the deepest recesses of our subconscious minds. Think of the constellations as archetypes, representing fundamental patterns of human experience – love, loss, ambition, fear. By understanding these stellar narratives, we begin to decipher the cryptic messages of our dreams, those nocturnal dramas staged within the theater of our minds. This connection isn't arbitrary; it's rooted in the ancient understanding of the interconnectedness of the cosmos and the human psyche. The macrocosm reflects the microcosm, as above, so below.

Consider the constellation of Orion, the Hunter. Often associated with strength, courage, and pursuit, its appearance in a dream might signify a quest, a pursuit of a goal, or the need to overcome obstacles. Perhaps you're facing a challenging situation in your waking life. Orion's presence in your dream could be a symbolic nudge to embrace your inner strength and pursue your objective with unwavering determination. Conversely, the constellation of Cassiopeia, the Queen, often represents vanity and arrogance. Her appearance might signal a need for introspection, a warning against excessive pride or self-centeredness. These stellar symbols act as mirrors, reflecting back aspects of ourselves we might not consciously recognize.

Interpreting the language of stars within the context of dreams requires more than simply identifying the constellations present. The context of the dream, the emotions you experienced, and the other symbols present all contribute to the overall meaning. For instance, a dream featuring the constellation Ursa Major, the Great Bear, might have different interpretations depending on the surrounding imagery. If the bear appears peaceful and nurturing, it might signify maternal protection or guidance. If the bear is aggressive or threatening, it could represent repressed anger or a feeling of being overwhelmed. Pay attention to the nuances. The stars whisper; they don't shout.

Furthermore, the brightness and position of the stars within a dream can also carry significance. A brightly shining star might represent hope, clarity, or a sudden insight. A dim or fading star could symbolize a loss of direction, fading hope, or a forgotten memory. The position of the stars in relation to each other can also offer clues. For instance, a cluster of stars forming a recognizable shape might signify a particular group of people or a specific situation in your life. The key is to observe, to pay attention to the subtle details, and to trust your intuition.

To truly understand the language of stars in your dreams, develop a personal lexicon. Keep a dream journal and note any celestial imagery that appears. Research the mythology and symbolism associated with each constellation and star. Reflect on how these symbolic meanings resonate with your personal experiences and emotions. Over time, you'll begin to recognize recurring patterns and develop a deeper understanding of your own unique dream language. This is a journey of self-discovery, a process of unveiling the hidden messages encoded within the celestial tapestry of your dreams.

Now, venture beyond the familiar constellations and explore the individual stars themselves. Sirius, the Dog Star, known for its brilliance, often signifies guidance and spiritual enlightenment. Betelgeuse, a red giant in Orion, can symbolize transformation and impending change due to its nearing supernova stage. Polaris, the North Star, a constant beacon in the night sky, often represents stability, direction, and a connection to one's true north. Each star holds a unique story, a specific energetic signature that can illuminate the hidden landscapes of your dreams.

Engage with the stars actively. Before you sleep, gaze at the night sky. Focus on a specific constellation or star that resonates with you. Ask for guidance and clarity in your dreams. Upon waking, record any dream imagery related to the stars. This practice strengthens the connection between your conscious mind and the subtle language of the cosmos. The stars offer a roadmap, a celestial guide to navigating the uncharted territories of the subconscious.

Don't limit your exploration to the traditional interpretations of the stars. Allow for personal associations and intuitive insights. A specific star or constellation might hold a unique meaning for you based on a personal experience or a significant memory. Trust your inner wisdom and allow your intuition to guide you in deciphering the symbolic messages of the stars. This isn't a rigid science; it's a fluid art of interpretation.

Finally, remember that the language of stars is not merely a tool for understanding dreams. It's a gateway to a deeper understanding of yourself, your connection to the cosmos, and the intricate interplay between the conscious and subconscious mind. The celestial tapestry is a reflection of the inner universe, a mirror reflecting the hidden depths of your being. By learning to read the language of the stars, you embark on a journey of self-discovery, unveiling the mysteries within and without. It's a journey of unveiling the hidden whispers of the cosmos, reflected in the dreams that shape your reality. The celestial sphere, when perceived through the lens of dreams, becomes a powerful instrument for self-knowledge.

3 Botanical Necromancy

The art of botanical necromancy hinges on understanding that death, in the natural world, is not an ending but a transformation. A fallen leaf nourishes the soil, feeding the roots of the tree from which it came. This cyclical dance of life and death, decay and rebirth, is the very essence of this practice. We don't seek to raise the dead in some grotesque mockery of life. Instead, we strive to commune with the lingering essence, the echo of a life once lived, held within the dried petals, the brittle stems, the dust of pollen. Within these remnants resides a unique energy, a whisper of the plant's experiences, its connection to the earth and the cosmos. Tapping into this energy allows us to gain insight into the unseen currents that flow through Willowbrook, connecting us to the whispers of its spectral inhabitants.

Harnessing this energy requires respect, reverence, and a deep understanding of the natural world. Forget Hollywood depictions of chanting over bubbling cauldrons. Botanical necromancy is a subtle art, a delicate dance between the practitioner and the spectral realm. We begin by selecting our botanical allies with careful consideration. Each plant holds its own unique properties, its own history and connection to the spiritual realm. Willow bark, for instance, with its association with grief and the moon, can be used to communicate with spirits tied to emotional trauma. Dried rosemary, symbolic of remembrance, might unlock memories trapped within the walls of Willowbrook. The choice of plant is paramount, shaping the nature of the communication and the insights we receive.

Preparation is key. The chosen plant material should be ethically sourced and harvested, preferably during a time of astrological significance relevant to the desired outcome. Drying the plant under specific conditions – perhaps in moonlight, or buried in earth for a specific number of days – further concentrates its spectral energy. Once prepared, the plant material can be used in various ways. Burning it as incense can release its essence into the air, creating an atmosphere conducive to communication. Infusing it in water creates a sacred wash, used to cleanse objects or spaces, removing energetic blockages and allowing the whispers of the past to surface. A poultice, made from crushed herbs and a binding agent, can be applied to specific locations on the body, acting as a conduit to heighten psychic sensitivity.

The environment plays a crucial role in botanical necromancy. Ideally, rituals should be performed outdoors, beneath the open sky, where the energies of the earth and cosmos can converge. Willowbrook's grounds, saturated with history and spectral resonance, offer a potent backdrop for such practices. Choose a location that feels energetically charged – perhaps near an ancient tree, a flowing stream, or a spot where the veil between worlds seems particularly thin. The time of day also matters. The twilight hours, the liminal spaces between day and night, are often considered most auspicious for spectral communication, as the boundaries between worlds blur.

More than simply selecting plants and performing rituals, botanical necromancy involves cultivating a deep connection with the natural world. It requires spending time in nature, observing the cycles of life and death, and developing an intuitive understanding of the subtle energies that permeate all living things. This connection, this empathy, is what allows us to truly hear the whispers of dead flora. It allows us to translate the rustling of dried leaves into meaningful messages, to decipher the secrets encoded in the patterns of decaying bark. It is through this deep listening that we begin to unravel the mysteries of Willowbrook's spectral circus.

This communication is not always direct, nor is it always easy to interpret. The whispers of dead flora are subtle, often veiled in symbolism and metaphor. They might manifest as fleeting images, intuitive feelings, or synchronicities in the physical world. A sudden gust of wind, an unexpected encounter with a specific animal, or a dream filled with vivid imagery – all of these can be messages from the spectral realm, conveyed through the medium of our chosen plant allies. Developing the ability to discern these subtle cues is a crucial aspect of botanical necromancy. It involves cultivating a quiet mind, a receptive heart, and a willingness to trust the whispers that come.

The "Green Grimoire" is not a physical book, but rather the accumulated knowledge and wisdom passed down through generations of practitioners. It is a living document, constantly evolving as we deepen our understanding of the natural world and its connection to the spectral realm. The knowledge within this grimoire is not confined to recipes and rituals. It encompasses a holistic understanding of the interconnectedness of all things, the delicate balance between life and death, and the profound power of nature to heal and transform.

Through careful observation and diligent practice, we learn to read the language of the natural world, to understand the messages encoded within the patterns of growth and decay. We learn to distinguish between the whisper of a willow and the sigh of a cypress, to understand the unique energetic signatures of different plants and their corresponding connections to the spectral realm. We learn to navigate the subtle nuances of energy, to sense the presence of unseen forces, and to interpret the messages they convey.

This journey of discovery is not for the faint of heart. It demands patience, perseverance, and a willingness to embrace the unknown. But for those who are willing to dedicate themselves to this path, the rewards are immeasurable. Botanical necromancy offers a profound connection to the natural world, a deeper understanding of the mysteries of life and death, and a unique perspective on the spectral realm that lies just beyond the veil of our everyday perception. In the context of Willowbrook, it offers a key to unlocking the secrets of the spectral circus, to deciphering the whispers that permeate its grounds, and to understanding the intricate interplay between the subconscious mind and the spectral realm.

3.1 Whispers of Dead Flora

The desiccated petals of a forgotten rose, brittle and brown, hold more than just the memory of a summer bloom. They whisper tales of bygone seasons, of sun-drenched afternoons and dew-kissed mornings, of the life that thrived before succumbing to the inevitable cycle of decay. Within their fragile forms lie echoes of the vital energies that once pulsed through stem and leaf, a silent testament to the ephemeral nature of existence. In the practice of botanical necromancy, these whispers become a language, a means of communication between the realms of the living and the spectral. To truly listen, one must cultivate a particular sensitivity, an attunement to the subtle vibrations that linger in the husks of departed flora. This chapter explores the art of interpreting these spectral murmurs, of gleaning wisdom and insight from the silenced voices of the botanical world.

The first step in this esoteric practice lies in the mindful selection of your botanical medium. Not every withered leaf or dried flower holds the same potency. Seek out specimens with a palpable history, plants that have witnessed significant events or absorbed the emotional resonance of their surroundings. A rose from a lover's grave, a sprig of rosemary from a forgotten garden, the gnarled root of a lightning-struck oak – each carries its own unique narrative, waiting to be unveiled. These are not merely dried remnants of life, but vessels imbued with residual energies, whispering secrets to those who know how to listen. Consider the environment in which the plant lived and died. A wildflower that bloomed in a meadow vibrates with a different frequency than a hothouse orchid, pampered and protected. The former whispers of untamed vitality, the latter of cultivated elegance. Once you have chosen your botanical subject, prepare a sacred space. This could be a secluded corner of your garden, a quiet room lit by candlelight, or any place where you feel a sense of connection to the unseen world. Clear the space of distractions, both physical and mental. Allow your mind to settle into a state of receptive stillness. Hold the chosen plant gently in your hands, focusing your attention on its texture, its fragrance, the delicate tracery of its veins. Visualize the life force that once animated it, the vibrant green of its leaves, the vibrant hues of its blossoms. Imagine the sun's warmth nourishing its growth, the rain's gentle kiss quenching its thirst. Breathe deeply, inhaling the essence of the plant's spectral memory, exhaling the anxieties and distractions of the mundane world.

As you deepen your connection with the chosen plant, begin to ask your questions. These should be framed with respect and reverence, acknowledging the spirit of the plant and the wisdom it holds. Phrase your inquiries with clarity and intention, focusing on specific aspects of Willowbrook's spectral circus that you wish to understand. Do not expect immediate, thunderous pronouncements. The whispers of dead flora are subtle, delicate, often veiled in symbolism and metaphor. Be patient and attentive, observing any sensations that arise within you – a subtle shift in temperature, a tingling in your fingertips, an image flashing before your mind's eye. These are the initial responses, the first stirrings of communication. Record these impressions in a journal, sketching images, noting down words or phrases that come to mind, however fragmented or seemingly nonsensical they may appear. Over time, these disparate fragments will begin to coalesce into a coherent narrative, revealing the hidden truths of Willowbrook's spectral past.

The practice of botanical necromancy is not merely about extracting information from the deceased. It is about forging a relationship with the natural world, recognizing the interconnectedness of all living things, even in death. It is about understanding the continuous cycle of life, death, and rebirth, and the wisdom that can be gleaned from each stage. By learning to listen to the whispers of dead flora, you gain access to a vast reservoir of knowledge, unlocking secrets that lie beyond the reach of the mundane senses. Through this practice, the spectral circus of Willowbrook becomes more than just a ghostly spectacle. It transforms into a mirror reflecting the hidden depths of your own subconscious, illuminating the intricate tapestry of dreams, memories, and forgotten emotions that shape your perception of reality. The delicate, decaying forms of dead flora become conduits, bridging the gap between the tangible and the intangible, guiding you deeper into the mysteries of Willowbrook and the enigmatic whispers that resonate within its spectral grounds. They become keys, unlocking the doors of perception and unveiling the hidden dimensions that lie just beyond the veil of ordinary consciousness. Through patient observation and dedicated practice, the silent language of dead flora can illuminate the path towards understanding the intricate relationship between the natural world, the human psyche, and the spectral realm that binds them together. It is a path that leads to the heart of Willowbrook's mysteries, where the whispers of the past intertwine with the echoes of the present, revealing the secrets of the spectral circus and the deeper truths of the human subconscious.

3.2 The Green Grimoire

The practice of botanical necromancy isn't about raising armies of vengeful shrubbery. It's a delicate art of listening to the whispers of deceased flora, a communion with the lingering essence of plant life to glean insights into the ethereal tapestry of Willowbrook. Forget the lurid imagery of Hollywood necromancers. Here, amidst the spectral circus, we engage with the subtle language of decay and rebirth. This practice requires a reverence for the natural world, a deep understanding of the cyclical nature of life and death, and, crucially, the ability to interpret the subtle signs and symbols embedded within the botanical realm. We seek not to control, but to understand, to learn from the echoes of life that linger within even the most desiccated leaf.

The first step involves creating a sanctuary, a space dedicated to this communion. Choose a location resonant with natural energy—perhaps a secluded corner of your garden, a space near a whispering willow, or even a quiet room adorned with dried herbs and flowers. Cleanse the area with fragrant smoke, preferably from sacred herbs like sage or rosemary. This purification ritual prepares the space, creating a neutral ground for communication. Your tools are simple: a mortar and pestle for grinding herbs, small bowls for offerings of spring water or honey, and a blank journal to record your observations. Remember, botanical necromancy isn't about elaborate rituals or incantations; it's about creating a space conducive to quiet contemplation and attuned listening.

Central to the practice is the creation of a "death tincture." This isn't a potion of decay, but a catalyst for connection. Gather petals from flowers that have died naturally, leaves that have fallen from the trees, and dried herbs symbolic of remembrance and transition. Steep these in pure spring water under the waning moon, allowing the essence of their past lives to infuse the water. This tincture will serve as both an offering and a tool for enhancing your sensitivity to the whispers of dead flora. As the tincture steeps, meditate upon the cyclical nature of life, the continuous dance of birth, growth, decay, and rebirth. Visualize the energy of the deceased plants mingling with the water, their stories slowly dissolving into the liquid.

Once the tincture is prepared, begin by selecting a plant you wish to commune with. It could be a dried flower from a cherished bouquet, a fallen leaf from a significant tree, or even a piece of wood from a willow within Willowbrook Estate. Hold the plant in your hand, close your eyes, and focus on its texture, its scent, its lingering energy. Imagine its life cycle, from seed to sprout, to full bloom, to eventual decay. Feel its story flowing through your fingertips. Anoint the plant with a few drops of the death tincture, whispering words of respect and gratitude. This offering acknowledges the plant's past life and invites its spirit to communicate.

Now comes the most crucial aspect of botanical necromancy: listening. Open your senses to the subtle cues around you. Don't expect grand pronouncements or ghostly apparitions. The whispers of dead flora are subtle—a gentle breeze rustling the leaves, a faint scent of decaying earth, a fleeting image flickering in your mind's eye. Record these impressions in your journal, noting any symbols, sensations, or emotions that arise. These seemingly random occurrences are the language of the deceased plants, fragments of their stories and insights into the spectral world. Deciphering this language requires patience, intuition, and an understanding of the symbolic language of nature.

The messages you receive may not be direct answers to your questions. They might be symbolic representations, fragments of memories, or glimpses into the past. For instance, a wilted rose petal might symbolize lost love, while a sturdy oak leaf might represent resilience. The interpretation of these symbols is subjective and depends on your intuition and the context of your inquiry. Cross-reference your observations with existing folklore, herbalism traditions, and your personal understanding of the plant's symbolism. This process of deciphering the whispers can reveal hidden connections between the spectral circus, the history of Willowbrook Estate, and the mysteries of the subconscious mind. Remember, botanical necromancy is not about conjuring spirits; it's about connecting with the lingering essence of plant life to gain a deeper understanding of the unseen world.

Through consistent practice and careful observation, you'll develop a heightened sensitivity to the whispers of dead flora. You'll begin to perceive the interconnectedness of all living things, the continuous flow of energy between the physical and spectral realms. Botanical necromancy provides a unique lens through which to explore the mysteries of Willowbrook Estate, allowing you to tap into the wisdom of the natural world and unravel the secrets of the spectral circus that haunts its grounds. This intimate connection with the botanical world can illuminate the hidden pathways of the subconscious, revealing the intricate dance between dreams, reality, and the whispers of the past.

4 Dreamscapes: Uncharted Realms

The tapestry of dreams, woven with the threads of our subconscious, stretches far beyond the familiar landscapes of waking life. It is a realm of infinite potential, where the laws of physics bend to the whims of our inner world, and the impossible becomes not only plausible, but vividly real. This is the uncharted territory of the dreamscape, a place where we encounter fragmented memories, suppressed desires, and the raw, unfiltered emotions that shape our being. To navigate these ethereal realms is to embark on a journey of self-discovery, a descent into the depths of our own minds. Within these swirling mists of imagination, we find ourselves face-to-face with the symbolic representations of our deepest fears and aspirations.

The architecture of dreams is fluid, shifting and reforming with the currents of our thoughts. One moment, you might find yourself in a grand ballroom, the next, traversing a desolate wasteland. These sudden transitions, while often disorienting, offer a glimpse into the associative nature of the subconscious. A familiar face might morph into a monstrous figure, reflecting hidden anxieties or unresolved conflicts. A cherished childhood toy might appear broken or distorted, symbolizing the loss of innocence or the passage of time. These seemingly random occurrences hold profound meaning, acting as cryptic messages from the depths of our being. Understanding the language of these symbols is crucial to unlocking the secrets held within our dreams.

Consider the recurring motif of the labyrinth. Often encountered in dreamscapes, the labyrinth represents the intricate pathways of the subconscious mind. Navigating its twisting corridors can be a frustrating and bewildering experience, reflecting the challenges we face in understanding our own inner workings. The feeling of being lost or trapped within a labyrinth often mirrors the sense of being overwhelmed by our emotions or grappling with complex personal issues. Yet, the labyrinth also holds the promise of discovery. Reaching the center can symbolize a breakthrough in self-awareness, a moment of clarity and understanding.

Further deepening the mystery of the dreamscape is the phenomenon of recurring dreams. These repetitive nocturnal narratives, often imbued with a heightened sense of urgency or emotional intensity, demand our attention. They represent unresolved issues, persistent fears, or deeply ingrained patterns of thought that continue to exert influence over our waking lives. By carefully examining the recurring elements and emotional undertones of these dreams, we can gain valuable insight into the underlying psychological dynamics that shape our behavior. They offer a unique opportunity to confront and process unresolved trauma, anxieties, and limiting beliefs. Through this process of introspection, we can begin to unravel the complex tapestry of our subconscious and integrate these fragmented aspects of ourselves.

And then there are the lucid dreams. These extraordinary experiences occur when the dreamer becomes aware that they are dreaming, gaining a degree of conscious control over the dream environment. In this state of heightened awareness, the dreamscape becomes a playground for exploration and self-discovery. The ability to manipulate the dream narrative allows for the direct confrontation of fears, the rehearsal of desired outcomes, and the exploration of creative potential. Lucid dreaming opens a portal to the deepest recesses of the subconscious, offering a powerful tool for personal growth and transformation. It allows us to interact with the symbolic representations of our inner world in a direct and meaningful way, providing a unique opportunity to resolve internal conflicts and reprogram limiting beliefs. This conscious engagement with the dream state can lead to profound insights and a deeper understanding of the intricate relationship between our conscious and subconscious minds. Through the practice of lucid dreaming, we gain the power to shape our inner landscapes and, in turn, influence the trajectory of our waking lives.

The journey through the dreamscape is not always a pleasant one. We may encounter shadowy figures that embody our deepest fears, relive traumatic experiences, or find ourselves trapped in nightmarish scenarios. These encounters, while unsettling, are essential for understanding the full spectrum of our subconscious. They offer a safe space to confront our demons, process unresolved emotions, and integrate the darker aspects of ourselves. By acknowledging and accepting these shadow aspects, we move towards a more complete and integrated sense of self. This journey into the depths of our subconscious is an ongoing process, a continuous exploration of the ever-evolving landscapes within. With each dream, we peel back another layer, uncovering new facets of ourselves and gaining a deeper appreciation for the intricate tapestry of our inner world. Through the careful examination of our dreams, we embark on a path of self-discovery, unlocking the hidden potential within and cultivating a more profound understanding of the human experience.

4.1 The Labyrinth of Sleep

Dreams. Elusive, ephemeral whispers from the depths of our being. They are not simply random firings of neurons, but intricate tapestries woven with the threads of our subconscious mind. To navigate the labyrinth of sleep is to embark on a journey into the uncharted territories of our inner selves, a realm where logic bends and the familiar dissolves into the surreal. This journey, however, is rarely straightforward. Like the twisting corridors of a mythical maze, dreams present us with dead ends, false paths, and shifting landscapes. One moment we might find ourselves soaring through the clouds, only to plummet the next into a shadowy abyss. Understanding the structure of this labyrinth is key to unlocking its mysteries.

Consider the dream's narrative arc. Often, dreams unfold as fragmented stories, a series of seemingly unconnected vignettes that defy rational explanation. Yet, within this chaos lies a hidden order, a symbolic language unique to the dreamer. The challenge lies in deciphering this language, peeling back the layers of metaphor and symbolism to reveal the underlying emotional currents. Think of recurring motifs – a specific place, a particular person, an object that appears time and again. These are not coincidences. They are breadcrumbs scattered by your subconscious, clues leading you deeper into the heart of the labyrinth. Examine the emotions evoked by these recurring elements. Fear, joy, anxiety, longing—these are the compass points guiding your exploration.

The labyrinth of sleep is not a static structure. It is constantly evolving, reshaping itself with each night's descent into slumber. Our experiences, our fears, our desires—all leave their imprint on the dream landscape. This dynamic nature makes mapping the labyrinth a continuous process, a lifelong journey of self-discovery. Think of a dream journal as your cartographer's toolkit. Recording your dreams, no matter how fragmented or bizarre, provides a tangible record of your subconscious explorations. Over time, patterns begin to emerge, revealing the recurring themes and symbols that populate your personal dream landscape. Note the details: colors, sounds, textures, even smells. These sensory impressions add depth and richness to the map, offering further insights into the underlying meaning of your dreams.

Furthermore, the architecture of the dream labyrinth can be influenced by external factors. The foods we eat, the medications we take, even the ambient noise in our sleeping environment can seep into our dreams, altering their form and content. Consider the impact of your waking life on your dream world. A stressful day at work might manifest as a frantic chase through a crowded city. A joyous celebration could translate into a dream of soaring flight. By becoming attuned to these connections, you gain a deeper understanding of the interplay between your conscious and subconscious minds. This awareness empowers you to navigate the labyrinth with greater clarity and purpose.

Beyond the personal labyrinth, consider the concept of the collective unconscious, a reservoir of shared archetypes and symbols that resonate across cultures and time. These universal motifs – the hero, the shadow, the anima/animus – can appear in our dreams, adding another layer of complexity to the labyrinth. Recognizing these archetypes allows us to tap into a deeper wellspring of meaning, connecting our individual experiences to a broader human narrative. Explore the work of Carl Jung, whose theories on the collective unconscious provide a valuable framework for interpreting dream symbolism. His work offers a rich tapestry of insights into the universal patterns that shape our inner worlds.

Finally, consider the possibility of shared dreams, those rare instances where two or more individuals dream the same or similar dream. This phenomenon suggests that the labyrinth of sleep may not be entirely personal, but can occasionally intersect with the dream worlds of others. While scientific understanding of shared dreams is limited, anecdotal evidence suggests that they often occur between individuals with strong emotional bonds. This raises intriguing questions about the nature of consciousness and the interconnectedness of our inner worlds. Could shared dreams be glimpses into a collective dream space, a shared dimension accessible through the labyrinth of sleep? This area of dream research remains largely unexplored, offering fertile ground for further investigation.

As you delve deeper into the labyrinth of sleep, remember that there is no single "correct" interpretation of your dreams. The meaning you ascribe to them is ultimately a personal one, shaped by your own unique experiences and perspectives. Embrace the mystery, the ambiguity, the inherent strangeness of the dream world. The labyrinth of sleep is not a puzzle to be solved, but a realm to be explored. It is a journey into the deepest recesses of your being, a journey that offers profound insights into the hidden landscapes of your soul. And like all worthwhile journeys, it is the process of exploration, not the destination, that holds the greatest rewards.

4.2   Shadows of the Subconscious

The subconscious, that vast, uncharted territory within us, holds the key to understanding the spectral circus of Willowbrook. It's a realm of shadows, a twilight zone where our deepest fears, repressed desires, and forgotten memories perform their eerie dance. Think of it as the backstage area of the conscious mind, where the props and costumes of our waking lives are stored, sometimes haphazardly, often revealing more than we intend. Within these shadows, the spectral circus finds its genesis, its performers drawn from the fragmented narratives and symbolic imagery of our inner world. We are, in a sense, the unwitting ringmasters of our own subconscious spectacles.

This shadowy realm isn't merely a repository of forgotten experiences. It's a dynamic, ever-shifting landscape, constantly being reshaped by the influx of new experiences and the subtle, ceaseless ebb and flow of our emotional tides. Imagine a subterranean river carving new pathways through the earth, its course dictated by the unseen forces of pressure and gravity. Similarly, our subconscious is molded by the pressures and pulls of our daily lives, our anxieties, our aspirations, our loves, and our losses, all leaving their indelible mark on its malleable form. Understanding this dynamic nature is crucial to navigating the labyrinthine corridors of Willowbrook and deciphering the whispers of its spectral inhabitants.

The shadows, however, are not inherently malevolent. They are, rather, a reflection of our wholeness, encompassing both the light and the darkness that resides within each of us. Like the moon, which reveals its different phases as it orbits the earth, our subconscious reveals different facets of our being depending on the angle from which it is illuminated by the conscious mind. Ignoring these shadows, pretending they don't exist, is akin to navigating a ship at night without consulting the stars. It leaves us vulnerable to unseen reefs and currents, tossed about by the unpredictable tides of our own inner world. Embracing the shadows, on the other hand, allows us to chart a more informed course, to navigate the complexities of our inner landscape with greater awareness and understanding.

To truly understand the spectral circus, one must delve into the language of the subconscious. This language isn't expressed in words or logical propositions, but in symbols, metaphors, and archetypes. Think of the recurring motifs that populate our dreams: the shadowy figure lurking in the periphery, the endless staircase leading nowhere, the feeling of being chased or falling. These are not random occurrences but rather symbolic representations of deeper psychological processes, messages from the subconscious trying to make themselves heard. They are the whispers of the willows, the phantom calliope's haunting melody, the silent tears of the spectral clowns. To decipher these messages, we must learn to interpret the symbolic language of our dreams, much like a cartographer deciphering the ancient symbols on a weathered map.

One powerful tool for exploring these subconscious shadows is dream journaling. By meticulously recording our dreams upon waking, we begin to discern patterns and recurring themes, the subtle threads that weave together the tapestry of our inner world. This process is akin to the meticulous charting of constellations, carefully mapping the positions and relationships of the celestial bodies in order to understand their influence on the terrestrial realm. Just as the stars tell a story of cosmic creation and evolution, our dreams tell a story of our personal evolution, our hopes, fears, and the unresolved conflicts that shape our waking lives. Dream journaling allows us to create a personal map of our subconscious, a guide to navigating the landscapes of Willowbrook and interpreting the whispers of its spectral circus.

Furthermore, active imagination can serve as a powerful tool for engaging with the subconscious. By consciously entering a state of reverie, we can interact with the symbolic figures and landscapes of our inner world. This is not merely daydreaming but a focused and deliberate exploration of the subconscious, much like the practice of botanical necromancy, where we commune with the spirits of deceased plants to gain insight into the unseen realms. Through active imagination, we can dialogue with the ringmaster of our inner circus, unravel the symbolism of the Freudian trapeze artists, and understand the silent sorrows of the spectral clowns. This allows us to gain a deeper understanding of the forces at play within our own minds and to integrate the wisdom of the subconscious into our conscious awareness. Finally, remember that the exploration of the subconscious is not a destination but a lifelong journey. The landscapes of our inner world are constantly shifting, evolving, and revealing new layers of meaning. Like the unending show of the spectral circus, the exploration of our subconscious is a continuous process of discovery, a dance between the shadows and the light. It is through this ongoing exploration that we come to a deeper understanding of ourselves, our place in the cosmos, and the whispers of the Willowbrook Estate.

4.3 Lucid Portals

The veil between the waking world and the dreamscape is thinner than most believe. It shimmers, distorts, and occasionally tears, allowing glimpses of the fantastical realm beyond. These tears, these fleeting moments of clarity within the dream, are what we call lucid portals. They offer not just a viewing platform into our subconscious, but a chance to actively participate in its unfolding narrative. Imagine the spectral circus of your own mind, the clowns, the ringmaster, the trapeze artists, all performing a play written by your deepest desires and fears. With lucidity, you become not merely an audience member, but a director, a stagehand, even a performer in this grand, oneiric production.

Cultivating this awareness within the dream state is no easy feat. It requires a diligent practice of self-observation both in waking life and within the dream itself. Begin by keeping a detailed dream journal. Record every fragment you can recall upon waking, no matter how insignificant it may seem. The very act of remembering and recording strengthens the connection between your conscious and subconscious mind. Look for recurring symbols, landscapes, and characters. These are the whispers of your inner world, trying to communicate their cryptic messages. As you become more attuned to these patterns, you'll begin to recognize them within the dream itself, triggering the spark of lucidity.

Reality testing is another crucial tool. Throughout your day, perform simple checks to confirm you're awake. Try pushing your finger through the palm of your other hand. In the waking world, this is, of course, impossible. But in the dream state, the laws of physics often bend to the whims of your subconscious. If your finger passes through your hand, you're likely dreaming. Make this a regular habit, and the same action performed within the dream can jolt you awake within it. This transition, this sudden awareness, is the opening of a lucid portal.

Once you find yourself standing within this portal, within the vibrant landscape of a lucid dream, the possibilities are boundless. You can explore the hidden corners of your subconscious, confront your deepest fears, and even rewrite the script of your dreams. Imagine flying over Willowbrook Estate, seeing the spectral circus from a new perspective. Converse with the clowns, unravel the secrets of the phantom calliope, and understand the silent tears they shed. The dream becomes a canvas upon which you can paint your desires, a stage upon which you can rehearse for waking life.

But tread carefully. The subconscious is a powerful and often unpredictable realm. While lucid dreaming can be a source of profound insight and personal growth, it can also be destabilizing if approached recklessly. Avoid the temptation to immediately control or manipulate the dream. Instead, begin by observing. Become familiar with the rules of this new reality. Note the subtle shifts in the landscape, the reactions of the dream characters to your presence. This respect for the dream environment will foster a sense of trust and allow you to navigate its depths with greater ease.

Furthermore, remember that the subconscious speaks in the language of symbolism. Don't take everything at face value. The spectral circus isn't just a random collection of phantoms. Each character, each act, represents a facet of your inner self. The ringmaster might symbolize a controlling aspect of your personality, while the trapeze artists could represent a desire for freedom and escape. By deciphering these symbols, you can gain a deeper understanding of your motivations, fears, and desires.

The journey to lucidity is a personal one. There's no single path that works for everyone. Experiment with different techniques, find what resonates with you, and be patient with the process. Some may find that certain herbs, used responsibly and with proper research, can facilitate vivid dreams and increase the likelihood of lucidity. Others may discover that meditation or visualization exercises before sleep enhance their dream recall. Keep exploring, keep practicing, and you'll find the keys to unlocking your own lucid portals, allowing you to step into the spectral circus of your subconscious and unravel the mysteries it holds.

Remember, the landscapes of our dreams are as vast and complex as the cosmos themselves. By learning to navigate them with awareness and intention, we gain access to a powerful tool for self-discovery and transformation. The whispers of the Willowbrook Estate, the echoes of its spectral circus, these are but reflections of the whispers within our own minds, waiting to be heard. Through the gateway of lucid dreaming, we can finally begin to listen.

4.4 Dream Weaver's Loom

The tapestry of dreams isn't merely observed; it's woven. Consider the threads: fragmented memories, suppressed desires, fears that skitter just beneath the surface of awareness. These are the raw materials of your nocturnal narratives. Imagine them unspooling from the cosmic spindle, spun into the vibrant, often bizarre, landscapes you traverse in your sleep. But what if you could grasp the spindle itself? What if you could consciously direct the weave, transforming the chaotic patterns into designs of your choosing? This is the art of dream weaving, the conscious manipulation of the oneiric landscape, and it's a skill honed through practice and understanding.

This isn't about simple lucid dreaming, though that's certainly a stepping stone. Lucidity is the awareness of dreaming, a flashlight in the shadowy corridors of your mind. Dream weaving, however, is taking hold of the architect's tools, reshaping the very structure of that corridor. It requires a deeper understanding of the symbolic language your subconscious speaks. Recall the spectral circus of Willowbrook, the phantom calliope's melody, the clowns' painted smiles concealing silent sorrows. These are not random apparitions, but manifestations of deeper psychological currents. By learning to decipher these symbols, you begin to understand the grammar of your dream world, the underlying logic that governs its often surreal manifestations.

Begin by meticulously documenting your dreams. Upon waking, seize the fleeting remnants before they dissolve like morning mist. Note the recurring motifs, the peculiar landscapes, the emotional undercurrents. This dream journal becomes your personal Rosetta Stone, translating the cryptic whispers of your subconscious into a language you can comprehend. Look for patterns, for connections between the symbols you encounter and your waking life. A recurring shadowed figure might represent a suppressed fear, a vast ocean a sense of overwhelm. As you decipher these connections, you gain a vocabulary with which to communicate with your dreaming self.

Once you understand the language, you can begin to shape the conversation. Before sleep, visualize the changes you wish to make in your dream landscape. Imagine yourself standing within the spectral big top, directing the ghostly performers, rewriting their script. Focus on the specific details – the colors of the costumes, the music of the calliope, the expressions on the clowns' faces. The more vivid your pre-sleep visualization, the more likely it is to manifest in your dreams. This is the first step towards active weaving, planting the seeds of intention in the fertile ground of your subconscious.

Don't be discouraged by initial failures. Like any craft, dream weaving requires patience and persistence. Your first attempts may be clumsy, the threads tangled and frayed. You might find yourself momentarily lucid, only to lose control and tumble back into the chaotic flow of the dream. But with each attempt, you refine your technique, strengthening your connection to the loom of your subconscious. You begin to recognize the subtle cues that signal a shift in the dream's narrative, learning to anticipate and even redirect the unfolding events.

As your skill develops, you can experiment with more complex manipulations. Imagine transforming the shadowy labyrinth of sleep into a sunlit garden, the echoes of loss into whispers of hope. Picture yourself conversing with the spectral figures, unraveling their cryptic pronouncements, even changing their roles in the ongoing dream drama. The possibilities are as vast as the imagination itself. By mastering the art of dream weaving, you're not just observing your dreams; you're actively participating in their creation, shaping the very fabric of your subconscious mind. This is a profound and empowering journey, one that can lead to deep self-discovery and personal transformation.

Through this process, the dream world becomes a sandbox for exploring your inner landscape. You can confront your fears in a safe environment, experiment with new identities, and even access hidden reservoirs of creativity. The insights gleaned from these dream explorations can then be integrated into your waking life, leading to greater self-awareness, emotional healing, and a deeper understanding of the complex interplay between the conscious and subconscious mind. The spectral circus, once a bewildering spectacle, becomes a canvas for self-expression, a playground for the soul. The loom of your dreams awaits. Take hold of the threads and begin to weave.

4.5 The Oneiric Oracle

The whispers of Willowbrook had always hinted at something more than just the rustling of leaves and the creaking of old timbers. A deeper current ran beneath the surface of the mundane, a tide of dreams pulling at the edges of reality. This current, this tide, flowed towards the heart of the spectral circus, a realm where the veil between waking and sleeping thinned to the point of translucence. Here, within this swirling kaleidoscope of fragmented memories and subconscious projections, lay the potential to tap into a powerful source of precognitive knowledge: the Oneiric Oracle.

Unlike the Delphic Oracle of ancient Greece, with its pronouncements shrouded in cryptic verse, the Oneiric Oracle speaks in the symbolic language of dreams. Its pronouncements are not delivered on stone tablets but woven into the tapestry of sleep, whispered on the wind of astral breezes, and painted onto the canvas of the night. To understand its pronouncements, we must learn to navigate this ethereal landscape, to decipher the cryptic whispers of the sleeping mind. This is not a task for the faint of heart, for the path to the Oneiric Oracle winds through shadowed valleys and across treacherous peaks of the subconscious. It demands an unwavering commitment to self-discovery and a willingness to confront the deepest recesses of one's own psyche.

The key to unlocking the wisdom of the Oneiric Oracle lies in the cultivation of what might be termed "oneiric literacy." This involves developing a keen awareness of the symbolic language of dreams – the recurring motifs, the bizarre juxtapositions, the emotionally charged narratives that populate our nights. Just as a cartographer charts the physical world, we must learn to chart the inner landscapes of our dreams, mapping the recurring symbols and themes that emerge from the depths of our subconscious. We must pay close attention to the emotional textures of our dreams, for these often hold crucial clues to their underlying meaning. A dream of flying, for instance, might symbolize a sense of liberation and empowerment, while a dream of falling might signify a fear of failure or loss of control.

Developing oneiric literacy requires a disciplined approach. A dream journal becomes our cartographer's tool, a place to meticulously record the details of our nocturnal journeys. Upon waking, before the tendrils of the dream dissipate into the morning mist, we should strive to capture as much detail as possible: the characters, the setting, the sequence of events, the prevailing emotions. Over time, patterns begin to emerge from the seemingly random chaos, revealing recurring symbols and themes that offer glimpses into the workings of our subconscious.

Once we begin to understand the language of our dreams, we can begin to engage with the Oneiric Oracle in a more conscious and deliberate way. We can formulate specific questions before sleep, focusing our intent on receiving guidance and insight. This is akin to posing a query to the ancient oracle, only the temple we enter is the inner sanctum of our own mind. The answers we receive may not always be clear or immediately understandable. They may come in the form of symbolic imagery, cryptic messages, or even visceral emotional experiences. The challenge lies in interpreting these dream pronouncements, in teasing out the underlying message concealed within the symbolic tapestry.

Remember, the Oneiric Oracle is not a fortune teller dispensing pre-packaged predictions. It does not offer a script for the future, but rather a roadmap for navigating the uncertain terrain of life. Its pronouncements are not fixed or immutable, but rather invitations to explore different possibilities, to consider alternative courses of action. The true power of the Oneiric Oracle lies not in its ability to predict the future, but in its capacity to illuminate the present, to reveal the hidden forces shaping our thoughts, feelings, and behaviors.

Through careful observation, meticulous journaling, and thoughtful interpretation, we can learn to decipher the whispers of the Oneiric Oracle. We can transform our dreams from fleeting fragments of the night into a powerful tool for self-discovery, personal growth, and spiritual transformation. The spectral circus, once a bewildering labyrinth of shadows and illusions, becomes a source of profound wisdom and insight, guiding us along the path towards a deeper understanding of ourselves and the world around us. The journey into the dreamscape, while often challenging, holds the promise of unveiling hidden truths and unlocking the vast potential that lies dormant within the sleeping mind. It is a journey worth undertaking for anyone seeking guidance and direction on the winding path of life. Embrace the whispers, heed the symbols, and the Oneiric Oracle will illuminate your way.

5 The Circus of the Subconscious

The subconscious mind, a swirling kaleidoscope of forgotten memories, suppressed desires, and nascent anxieties, finds a peculiar, if unsettling, expression in the spectral circus of Willowbrook. Imagine this: a silent big top materializing in the moonlit gardens, its ethereal canvas shimmering with an otherworldly luminescence. Within, spectral performers enact a bizarre pantomime, a distorted reflection of the inner turmoil churning beneath the surface of our conscious minds. This isn't mere entertainment; it's a deeply personal drama staged by the very fabric of our being.

These phantom players, the clowns with painted smiles concealing silent screams, the trapeze artists defying gravity with impossible grace, the strongman bending bars of iron will – they are not external entities. They are projections, symbolic representations of the forces at play within us. Consider the Ringmaster, a shadowy figure wielding a whip of subconscious commands. He represents the ego, striving to maintain order amidst the chaotic whirlwind of inner drives. His control, however, is tenuous, constantly threatened by the unruly impulses of the id, embodied by the mischievous clowns who disrupt the carefully orchestrated performance. The clowns, with their exaggerated features and grotesque antics, represent the primal urges that lurk beneath the veneer of civilized behavior. Their laughter echoes the unsettling realization that beneath the surface of composure lies a primal chaos.

The high-wire act, a delicate balancing act between conscious awareness and the abyss of the unknown, mirrors our own precarious navigation through the complexities of life. The tightrope walker, poised between two worlds, embodies the struggle to maintain equilibrium amidst the conflicting demands of internal desires and external pressures. Each step forward is a precarious gamble, a testament to the constant negotiation between our inner and outer realities. One misstep, one falter in concentration, and the carefully constructed facade crumbles, plunging us into the depths of the unconscious.

This spectral circus is not a fixed entity, but a fluid, ever-changing reflection of the individual's internal landscape. The acts morph and shift, the performers change their guises, mirroring the dynamic nature of the subconscious itself. For some, the dominant theme might be a fear of failure, represented by a perpetually failing tightrope walker. For others, it could be an unfulfilled desire for connection, symbolized by a lonely clown searching for an audience. The symbolism is deeply personal, a cryptic language whispered by the inner self.

To decipher this enigmatic language, we must delve into the rich tapestry of symbolic representation. The costumes, the music, the very setting itself, hold clues to the hidden meanings embedded within the performance. The gaudy colors of the clowns' attire might suggest suppressed joy, while the melancholic melody of the phantom calliope hints at underlying sadness. Every detail, however seemingly insignificant, contributes to the overall narrative unfolding within the spectral big top.

The spectral circus, though unnerving, offers a unique opportunity for self-discovery. By observing the performance closely, by paying attention to the subtle nuances of the acts, we can gain valuable insights into the workings of our own subconscious minds. It's a process of deciphering the symbolic language of dreams, of understanding the whispers of the willow trees that surround the estate, of connecting the celestial charts to the map of our inner selves. The process may be challenging, even frightening at times, but the rewards are immeasurable.

Just as the cartography of the cosmos helps us navigate the vast expanse of the universe, understanding the symbolism of the spectral circus provides a map to the uncharted territories within. It's a journey into the heart of our own being, a confrontation with the shadows that lurk within. Through this exploration, we can begin to integrate these hidden aspects of ourselves, bringing them into the light of conscious awareness. This integration is essential for personal growth and wholeness.

Remember, the spectral circus is not a place of judgment, but a realm of revelation. It doesn't condemn our hidden desires or anxieties, but rather presents them for our consideration. By acknowledging these aspects of ourselves, we can begin to understand their influence on our thoughts, feelings, and behaviors. This understanding is the first step towards healing and transformation. The spectral circus, then, becomes not a source of fear, but a powerful tool for self-discovery and empowerment. It offers a glimpse into the hidden machinery of the self, a chance to understand the forces that shape our lives. Embrace the whispers of the willows, listen to the silent tears of the clowns, and uncover the secrets of the subconscious mind.

5.1   The Ringmaster's Mind

The spectral circus is not merely a random assortment of phantasms; it possesses a distinct structure, a hierarchy. This implies a governing intelligence, a director, a ringmaster. This entity, however, is not a separate being pulling strings from behind a velvet curtain. Instead, consider it the focal point of a collective dream, the epicenter of Willowbrook's psychic residue. It is the personification of the estate's subconscious, a confluence of memories, emotions, and unresolved energies. Think of it as the conductor of an orchestra, weaving together the disparate instruments – the clowns, the trapeze artists, the strongmen – into a unified, albeit unsettling, symphony. This ringmaster doesn't exist in a physical sense, but as a psychic construct, a nexus of the collective unconscious of all who have lived, loved, and lost within Willowbrook's grounds.

This ringmaster's mind, therefore, is not a singular entity, but a multifaceted lens through which Willowbrook's history refracts. It is a kaleidoscope of fractured narratives, a palimpsest of overlapping experiences. The laughter of children echoes alongside the hushed whispers of lovers, punctuated by the cries of grief and the chilling silence of trauma. Each individual who has touched Willowbrook has, in a way, contributed a brushstroke to this swirling canvas of consciousness. Deciphering this tapestry requires not merely observation, but a deep dive into the symbolic language of the subconscious. It is a language whispered through the rustling willow branches, the creaking floorboards of the manor, and the mournful strains of the phantom calliope. Understanding this language is key to unlocking the secrets of the spectral circus.

To truly grasp the ringmaster's mind, we must embrace the concept of psychic resonance. Just as a tuning fork vibrates at a specific frequency, so too does Willowbrook resonate with the psychic energies of its past. These vibrations, like ripples in a pond, extend outward, influencing the dreams and perceptions of those who venture within its sphere of influence. Consider the spectral circus as a reflection of these psychic ripples, a visual manifestation of Willowbrook's collective subconscious. The more attuned you are to these subtle energies, the more clearly you will perceive the intricacies of the ringmaster's mind. It's not about seeing, but feeling the weight of history, the echoes of emotion that linger in the air.

Imagine the ringmaster's mind as a vast, uncharted ocean. The surface may appear calm, but beneath the waves, currents of emotion and memory swirl and collide. These subsurface currents are the true driving forces of the spectral circus. They dictate the movements of the performers, the tempo of the music, the very atmosphere of the big top. To navigate this psychic ocean, you must learn to interpret its subtle shifts and flows. This requires a sensitivity to the nuances of dream symbolism and an understanding of the language of the subconscious. Much like a seasoned sailor reads the wind and waves, you must learn to decipher the whispers of the willow trees and the phantom laughter echoing through the empty halls of the manor.

The ringmaster's mind is a constantly evolving entity, shaped by both the past and the present. As new individuals interact with Willowbrook, their experiences add new layers to its psychic tapestry. This dynamic interplay between the past and the present keeps the spectral circus in a state of perpetual flux, ensuring that its mysteries remain forever elusive. Like a river carving new paths through the earth, the collective unconscious of Willowbrook is constantly reshaping itself. This fluidity makes understanding the ringmaster's mind a continuous process, a journey of discovery rather than a destination. Therefore, each encounter with the spectral circus presents a unique opportunity to glimpse into the ever-shifting depths of Willowbrook's soul.

To interact with the ringmaster's mind effectively, you must adopt a mindset of receptivity. Rather than trying to impose your will upon the spectral circus, allow yourself to be guided by its subtle currents. Embrace the ambiguity, the uncertainty. The answers you seek are not readily apparent, but woven into the fabric of the experience itself. Think of it as learning a new language. You must first listen, absorb the rhythms and intonations, before you can begin to understand the meaning of the words. Similarly, to truly comprehend the ringmaster's mind, you must immerse yourself in the spectral circus, allowing its whispers to guide you through its labyrinthine depths.

Finally, remember that the ringmaster's mind is not a benevolent force. It is a repository of both light and shadow, joy and sorrow. While it may offer glimpses of profound insight, it also harbors the potential for deception and manipulation. Approach it with caution, respect, and a healthy dose of skepticism. The spectral circus is a reflection of the human psyche in all its complexity. It is a realm of beauty and terror, wisdom and madness. To truly understand the ringmaster's mind, you must be willing to confront not only the wonders of Willowbrook, but also its deepest, darkest secrets. This journey is not for the faint of heart, but for those who dare to explore the uncharted landscapes of the subconscious mind.

5.2 Freudian Trapeze Artists

The trapeze artists of Willowbrook's spectral circus, with their gravity-defying feats and painted smiles, are far more than mere phantoms. They embody the volatile, often paradoxical nature of the subconscious, swinging between repressed desires and anxieties. Through a Freudian lens, their acrobatic displays transform into a symbolic language, whispering secrets of the mind. Consider the daring leaps between platforms, a precarious dance between the conscious and unconscious. This mirrors the mind's constant negotiation between the world we present to others and the hidden landscape within. Each successful catch represents a fleeting moment of equilibrium, a temporary truce in the internal struggle. However, the inherent risk, the ever-present possibility of a fall, underscores the fragility of this balance. The trapeze, a slender bar suspended in the ethereal air, becomes a metaphor for the ego, constantly striving for stability amidst the competing forces of the id and superego.

The vibrant costumes, shimmering under the spectral big top, further illuminate this intricate psychic drama. The bold colours and exaggerated designs amplify the performative nature of the ego, masking the deeper, more primal impulses churning beneath. The sequins and feathers serve as distractions, a dazzling façade meant to conceal the raw emotions and unresolved conflicts simmering just below the surface. Look closely at the masks they wear. These painted smiles, frozen in an expression of perpetual joy, become ironic symbols of repressed sorrow. They highlight the discrepancy between external presentation and internal reality, a hallmark of the Freudian understanding of the psyche. The clowns, often seen as figures of amusement, take on a new, poignant significance. Their exaggerated gestures and slapstick routines become a defense mechanism, a way of deflecting attention from the underlying sadness and despair that haunt the subconscious.

Observe the dynamics between the trapeze artists. The intricate choreography, demanding precise timing and unwavering trust, reflects the delicate interplay between different facets of the personality. Each performer relies on the others, their individual actions contributing to a larger, interconnected whole. This interdependence highlights the complex network of relationships within the psyche, the constant push and pull between opposing forces. A missed catch, a stumble, a moment of hesitation, can disrupt the entire performance, just as a single unresolved conflict can throw the psyche into turmoil. The audience, unseen but ever-present, becomes a stand-in for the external world, the judging gaze that shapes and influences the ego's performance. The cheers and applause represent the validation sought by the conscious mind, while the silences and gasps reflect the anxieties and fears that lurk within.

Consider the very act of flying through the air, a defiance of gravity and earthly constraints. This symbolizes the yearning for liberation from the confines of the conscious mind, a desire to escape the limitations of logic and reason. The trapeze artists, suspended between heaven and earth, embody this yearning for transcendence, for a glimpse into the boundless realm of the unconscious. Their aerial ballet becomes a symbolic journey into the depths of the psyche, a daring exploration of the hidden desires and fears that shape our waking lives. Their breathtaking feats of daring, seemingly impossible from a grounded perspective, represent the boundless potential of the subconscious, a realm where the ordinary rules of physics and logic no longer apply. The fluidity of their movements, the effortless grace with which they navigate the ethereal space, speaks to the inherent dynamism of the unconscious, a world in constant flux, forever shifting and transforming.

The rhythmic swing of the trapeze, back and forth, mimics the cyclical nature of psychic processes. The repetitive motion suggests the recurring patterns of thought and behavior that often dominate the subconscious. These ingrained patterns, often rooted in childhood experiences, continue to exert a powerful influence on our adult lives, shaping our perceptions and influencing our choices. The trapeze, a physical embodiment of these repetitive patterns, becomes a tool for understanding the cyclical nature of the subconscious, the way in which unresolved conflicts and repressed emotions can resurface and manifest in our waking lives. The height of the swing, the point at which the trapeze reaches its apex, represents the peak of emotional intensity, the moment of greatest vulnerability and exposure. The descent, the inevitable return to the starting point, signifies the cyclical nature of these emotional experiences, the way in which they ebb and flow, rising and falling like the tides. By understanding these cyclical patterns, we can begin to unravel the complex tapestry of the subconscious, gaining insight into the hidden forces that shape our thoughts, emotions, and behaviors.

6 Willowbrook's Spectral History

The air at Willowbrook hung heavy, thick with the scent of decaying leaves and the faint, metallic tang of old blood. Not the vibrant, crimson blood of recent trauma, but the aged, rust-colored stain of a history long buried. This chapter delves into the heart of Willowbrook's spectral history, exploring the echoes of laughter and loss that cling to the estate like cobwebs. We begin by peeling back the layers of time, revealing the lives and tragedies that painted the canvas of this haunted landscape.

Willowbrook Estate was not always a place of shadows and whispers. It once thrived as a vibrant hub of social life, owned by the eccentric Valerius family. Elias Valerius, a flamboyant showman with a penchant for the peculiar, transformed the estate grounds into a private circus in the late 1800s. He filled it with exotic animals, dazzling performers, and a custom-built calliope whose melodies drifted across the countryside. The laughter of children, the gasps of astonished audiences, and the roar of the crowd filled the air. Willowbrook became synonymous with joy, a beacon of merriment in an otherwise ordinary world. But this golden age was tragically short-lived. A devastating fire, sparked by a faulty gas lamp during a late-night performance, swept through the big top, claiming the lives of many performers and guests, including Elias's wife and young daughter. The joy that once permeated Willowbrook was extinguished in a single, horrific night.

The phantom calliope's melody, once a symbol of Willowbrook's vibrant past, now serves as a haunting reminder of the tragedy. Its ethereal tunes, often heard drifting through the deserted grounds at twilight, are said to be a lament, a mournful cry echoing the loss and despair of that fateful night. Some claim the melodies shift and change, sometimes mimicking the playful tunes of the circus's heyday, only to descend into a dissonant, chaotic cacophony, reflecting the terror and confusion of the fire. Local folklore whispers that the calliope itself is possessed by the spirit of Elias Valerius, forever searching for his lost loved ones amidst the charred remains of his dreams. This melancholic music adds another layer to the spectral tapestry of Willowbrook, a constant, chilling reminder of the joy that was consumed by the flames. Attempts to locate the source of the music have all proved futile, adding to the mystery and solidifying its spectral nature.

The spectral clowns, once symbols of laughter and lightheartedness, now wander the grounds, their painted smiles a grotesque mockery of their former selves. These are not the jovial tricksters of childhood memories, but tragic figures, their silent tears reflecting the profound sorrow that permeates Willowbrook. Their white faces, once vibrant with color, are now streaked with ghostly trails, perhaps mimicking the soot and ash of the fire. They move with a slow, deliberate sadness, their movements a pantomime of grief. They are the embodiment of the duality of the human experience – the juxtaposition of laughter and sorrow, joy and despair. One story, passed down through generations of locals, tells of a young boy who wandered onto the estate grounds and encountered a group of spectral clowns. They silently offered him a wilted flower, its petals blackened and brittle, before vanishing into the mist. The boy, forever marked by the encounter, claimed he could feel the weight of their sorrow, the silent scream of their unspoken grief.

The echoes of laughter and loss intertwine within the very fabric of Willowbrook Estate, creating a spectral tapestry woven with joy and sorrow. The phantom calliope plays its mournful melodies, a constant reminder of the tragedy that befell the circus. The spectral clowns, their painted smiles a mask of grief, wander the grounds, silent witnesses to the horrors of the past. These elements combine to form a chilling yet poignant narrative, a testament to the enduring power of memory and the indelible mark left by both joy and sorrow on the landscape of the human heart. Willowbrook stands as a stark reminder that even in the darkest of shadows, echoes of the past persist, whispering their stories to those who dare to listen. They serve as a constant reminder that the human experience is a complex interplay of light and darkness, laughter and tears, and that even in the face of unimaginable loss, the echoes of joy can still be heard, faintly whispering in the wind.

6.1 Echoes of Laughter & Loss

The grand house, Willowbrook Estate, stood as a testament to a bygone era. Its weathered facade, etched with the passage of time, concealed a rich tapestry of joy and sorrow, laughter and tears. Ivy, a relentless climber, scaled the walls, its tendrils weaving through broken window panes like inquisitive fingers probing the past. Here, within these decaying walls, whispers of forgotten laughter echoed through dusty corridors, a chilling counterpoint to the pervasive silence. The estate's history wasn't simply etched in stone and wood, but also in the very air itself, a palpable presence that clung to the shadows.

Willowbrook had once been the vibrant heart of a thriving community. Summer evenings were filled with the joyous shrieks of children playing hide-and-seek amongst the rose bushes and the melodic murmur of conversations carried on the gentle breeze. Grand balls, opulent and extravagant, lit up the house like a beacon of festivity, drawing visitors from miles around. Music spilled from open windows, intertwining with the scent of jasmine and the intoxicating aroma of fine wines. The estate pulsed with life, a vibrant microcosm of human experience.

The central figure in Willowbrook's golden age was Elias Thorne, a charismatic entrepreneur with a penchant for the theatrical. He was a dreamer, a man captivated by the allure of the strange and the fantastical. His passions manifested in the creation of a private circus, a whimsical troupe of performers who brought joy to all who witnessed their spectacle. Acrobats defied gravity with breathtaking feats of agility, clowns painted smiles on the faces of children, and the ringmaster, Elias himself, orchestrated the chaos with a flourish of his cane. This circus was more than just entertainment; it was an extension of Elias's own vibrant spirit, a testament to his belief in the power of dreams and imagination.

However, as the seasons turned, a shadow began to creep across Willowbrook's sunlit facade. Tragedy struck in the form of a devastating fire, an inferno that consumed not only the grand ballroom but also the lives of many of the circus performers. Elias, consumed by grief and guilt, retreated into himself, the laughter that had once filled his life replaced by a haunting silence. The vibrant colours of the circus faded, replaced by the somber hues of loss and despair. The laughter echoing through the halls became a distorted, mournful sound, a chilling reminder of what had been lost.

The grounds became overgrown, the once meticulous gardens choked by weeds, mirroring the neglect within Elias's own heart. The spectral remnants of the circus began to manifest, their ethereal performances a macabre echo of the past. The joyous laughter of children morphed into chilling whispers, the vibrant music of the calliope into a mournful dirge. The fire, it seemed, had not only consumed lives but also released something else, something darker, into the very fabric of Willowbrook.

Over the years, stories of Willowbrook's haunting spread throughout the surrounding towns. The estate became a place of whispered legends, a testament to the enduring power of grief. Locals spoke of ghostly figures glimpsed through the decaying windows, the faint strains of spectral music carried on the wind, and the chilling echoes of laughter that seemed to mock the silence of the grave. The grounds themselves became a focal point for these spectral manifestations, the gnarled trees and overgrown pathways whispering tales of the past.

The story of Willowbrook Estate is a poignant exploration of the human condition, a reminder that even in the grandest of settings, joy and sorrow are often intertwined. It serves as a cautionary tale of the fragility of happiness and the enduring power of loss. The laughter that once echoed through the halls has been replaced by a haunting silence, a chilling reminder that even the most vibrant dreams can turn into nightmares. The echoes of the past, however, continue to resonate, whispering secrets to those who dare to listen. The spectral circus performs on, a ghostly reminder of a time when laughter filled the air, a time now lost to the shadows of Willowbrook's tragic past. The whispers remain, faint yet persistent, a haunting testament to the lives lived and lost within those crumbling walls. They are the echoes of a dream shattered, a reminder that even the brightest lights can be extinguished by the cold hand of fate. And in the silence that follows, the whispers remain, a ghostly chorus of laughter and loss, forever intertwined in the spectral history of Willowbrook Estate.

6.2 The Phantom Calliope

The melodies, warped and mournful, snaked through the skeletal willows, clinging to the decaying grandeur of Willowbrook Estate. They were the whispers of a forgotten carnival, a spectral symphony played on an unseen calliope, its keys pressed by ghostly fingers. This phantom instrument, the heart of the spectral circus, pulsated with a melancholic energy that permeated every corner of the estate. Its music was more than just sound; it was a psychic resonance, a siren's call luring the unwary deeper into the labyrinthine corridors of the subconscious. This chapter seeks to understand the significance of this phantom calliope, exploring its ethereal melodies as a key to unlocking the secrets of Willowbrook's spectral history.

The calliope's music seemed to shift and change depending on the listener's emotional state. Joyful memories could twist into grotesque parodies, underscored by a discordant, mocking tune. Conversely, moments of grief and despair were sometimes met with an almost comforting melody, a lullaby from the spectral realm. This empathetic quality of the music hinted at a deeper connection between the calliope and the subconscious minds of those within Willowbrook's influence. It suggested the instrument wasn't simply playing music, but weaving a narrative tailored to the listener's inner world, reflecting and amplifying their deepest fears and desires. This personalization of the music intensified its power, turning it from a mere auditory phenomenon into a potent psychological tool.

Local legends offered fragmented glimpses into the calliope's origins. Some whispered of a heartbroken circus musician, his soul bound to the instrument after a tragic accident beneath the big top. Others spoke of a malevolent entity, using the calliope to lure unsuspecting souls into its spectral domain. These disparate accounts, while lacking concrete evidence, painted a picture of an object steeped in both sorrow and a subtle, unnerving power. They provided a framework for understanding the calliope's role within the larger narrative of the spectral circus, suggesting a nexus point between the tangible and intangible realms.

Examining the decaying physical structure of Willowbrook Estate itself revealed intriguing clues. Within the remnants of a once-grand ballroom, a faded mural depicted a vibrant circus scene. At its center, a calliope, almost identical to the one heard in the spectral melodies, stood bathed in an otherworldly light. This discovery reinforced the connection between the estate's physical space and the spectral circus, suggesting the two were inextricably intertwined. The mural, a tangible echo of the ethereal circus, acted as a bridge between past and present, hinting at the possibility of uncovering further physical evidence within Willowbrook's grounds. It invited a deeper exploration of the estate's architecture and its potential role in amplifying or containing the calliope's power.

Through the application of botanical necromancy, using the withered remnants of roses once cultivated in Willowbrook's gardens, a faint psychic imprint was detected. It revealed a fragmented vision of a lavish party, music swirling through the air, guests dancing under the glow of chandeliers. Suddenly, the scene shifted, the music warping into a dissonant shriek as a shadowy figure emerged from the midst of the revelers. Though incomplete, this vision offered a glimpse into the moment the calliope's music took on its spectral quality, marking a turning point in Willowbrook's history. The roses, silent witnesses to the past, provided a crucial piece of the puzzle, linking the calliope's transformation to a specific event, and further implicating the estate's history in the spectral circus's manifestation.

The calliope's music served as a constant reminder of the unseen forces at play within Willowbrook. It acted as a conduit, channeling the emotional energy of the spectral circus and broadcasting it throughout the estate. This pervasive influence subtly manipulated the dreams of those who slept within Willowbrook's walls, weaving fragments of the spectral circus into their subconscious narratives. The calliope's melodies, far from being random notes, became a form of psychic programming, shaping the dream landscapes and perpetuating the cycle of fear and wonder that defined the estate. It was the soundtrack to a waking nightmare, blurring the lines between reality and the spectral realm.

By understanding the phantom calliope's role within the broader context of Willowbrook Estate's spectral history, one could begin to unravel the deeper mysteries of the subconscious mind. The calliope wasn't just a haunted instrument; it was a symbol of the power of unresolved emotions and the enduring influence of the past. Its haunting melodies, echoing through the decaying grandeur of Willowbrook, were a constant invitation to confront the shadows within and explore the uncharted landscapes of dreams. It was a key, albeit a spectral one, to unlocking the secrets that lay hidden within the subconscious, and ultimately, to understanding the true nature of the spectral circus itself.

6.3 The Clowns' Silent Tears

Beneath the greasepaint and exaggerated smiles, the spectral clowns of Willowbrook Estate harbor a profound sorrow. Their painted grins, frozen in a rictus of forced merriment, serve as masks concealing a deep well of melancholic energy. This chapter delves into the heart of their silent tears, uncovering the tragic histories that bind them to the ethereal circus and the estate itself. Each clown's story is a fragment of Willowbrook's past, a whisper carried on the phantom calliope's mournful tune. They are not merely entertainers in a spectral show; they are embodiments of forgotten joys and unprocessed grief, trapped in an endless cycle of performance.

One such clown, known only as "Chuckles," was once a flesh-and-blood performer, a beloved fixture of the traveling circuses that frequently visited Willowbrook in its heyday. His real name, Bartholomew, faded with time, swallowed by the persona he so meticulously crafted. Bartholomew's laughter was genuine, a beacon of light for children and weary adults alike. However, a tragic accident during a high-wire act, witnessed by a horrified crowd, claimed his life. His spirit, unable to sever its connection to the place where he found his greatest joy and his ultimate demise, became tethered to Willowbrook. Now, as Chuckles, he performs his spectral routine, a haunting echo of the laughter he once shared. The vibrancy of his painted smile starkly contrasts with the palpable sorrow emanating from his spectral form, a silent testament to a life cut short.

Another figure, "Weeps," a petite clown with perpetually flowing tears painted down her white face, mirrors a different kind of tragedy. In life, she was Elara, a young woman who dreamt of a life beyond Willowbrook's confines. Bound by familial obligations and societal expectations, her spirit withered beneath the weight of unspoken desires. Her only solace was the visiting circus, a fleeting glimpse into a world of freedom and self-expression. Upon her untimely death, Elara's unfulfilled dreams manifested in the form of Weeps, a poignant symbol of repressed emotions and the quiet desperation of a life unlived. Her painted tears are not mere stage makeup, but the physical manifestation of a heart perpetually breaking.

The spectral clowns are not simply individual tragedies, but a collective representation of a deeper sorrow. They are a reflection of the estate's history, absorbing the residue of joyous celebrations, bitter betrayals, and heart-wrenching losses that have unfolded within its walls. The vibrant colors of their costumes and the exaggerated nature of their performances serve as a distraction, a veil obscuring the profound sadness that permeates their spectral forms. Their silence amplifies their suffering, a ghostly chorus of unspoken grief echoing through the grounds of Willowbrook. They represent the hidden pain that often lurks beneath the surface of laughter, a reminder that even in the midst of joy, sorrow can find a foothold.

Exploring the individual stories of these spectral clowns is akin to peeling back the layers of Willowbrook's history. Their performances are not random acts of ghostly entertainment. They are meticulously choreographed reenactments of significant events, both joyous and tragic, played out in a never-ending loop. For instance, "Sparkles," a clown perpetually juggling flaming torches, represents the lavish parties once held within the estate. The fiery spectacle, however, is tinged with melancholy, reflecting the eventual decline of the family fortune and the bitter feuds that tore it apart.

Similarly, "Whispers," a mime with hauntingly expressive eyes, embodies the secrets and unspoken truths that have saturated Willowbrook's walls. His silent movements, imbued with a spectral grace, convey the weight of untold stories, hinting at forbidden romances, familial betrayals, and the silent suffering of those who lived and died within the estate.

Understanding the silent tears of the clowns requires not just observation, but empathy. By connecting with their stories, we can unlock deeper layers of Willowbrook's history and the complex relationship between the living and the spectral. Their silent performances serve as a reminder that every laugh, every tear, every experience leaves an indelible mark, shaping not only our individual lives but the very fabric of the places we inhabit.

The spectral clowns of Willowbrook are not mere figments of a haunted imagination. They are guides, leading us through the labyrinthine corridors of the estate's past. Their silent tears serve as a testament to the enduring power of human emotion, reminding us that even in the afterlife, the echoes of laughter and loss continue to resonate. By understanding their stories, we can gain a deeper understanding of the intricate tapestry of human experience and the profound connection between the living and the departed. They are a poignant reminder that even in the darkest corners of our dreams and subconscious, the potential for profound connection and understanding remains. Through their silent tears, the clowns invite us to explore the shadowed depths of Willowbrook and confront the spectral echoes of our own unspoken emotions.

7   Epilogue: Beyond the Veil

The whispers of Willowbrook Estate no longer echo with the same dissonant cacophony. The chaotic symphony of the spectral circus, once a bewildering torrent of sights and sounds, has begun to fade, leaving behind a quiet hum resonating with newfound understanding. The journey through the estate's haunted grounds, the exploration of celestial charts and the whispers of dead flora, has yielded a profound shift in perception. The veil between the conscious and subconscious, once an impenetrable barrier, now feels like a gossamer curtain, occasionally swaying to reveal glimpses of the profound interplay between our inner and outer worlds. We have navigated the astral plane, deciphered the language of stars, and confronted the shadows within the labyrinth of sleep.

This altered perception extends beyond the confines of Willowbrook. The celestial tapestry itself seems to shimmer with a different light. A new constellation has emerged, not visible to the naked eye, but discernible within the landscape of the soul. It is a constellation formed not of distant suns and swirling nebulae, but of the insights gleaned from our journey. Each star represents a fragment of understanding, a piece of the puzzle that is the human psyche. The fear and confusion that once clouded our vision have dissipated, replaced by a sense of clarity, a deep knowing that we are intrinsically connected to the cosmos, both within and without. This constellation, unique to each individual who undertakes the journey, serves as a personal guide through the uncharted territories of the subconscious. It is a testament to the transformative power of confronting our inner demons and embracing the totality of our being.

The echoes of laughter and loss, once so poignant within Willowbrook's walls, now carry a different timbre. The phantom calliope's melody, once a mournful dirge, now hints at a nascent hope. The clowns' silent tears, a symbol of repressed sorrow, have begun to evaporate, leaving behind a sense of quiet acceptance. Just as the earth absorbs the fallen leaves, enriching the soil for new growth, so too have we integrated the lessons learned from the spectral circus. The seeds of this experience, planted deep within the subconscious, promise a harvest of self-discovery and personal transformation. We have witnessed the Freudian trapeze artists, understood the ringmaster's mind, and in doing so, gained a deeper understanding of the forces that shape our thoughts, emotions, and dreams. This understanding allows us to tend the garden of our minds, nurturing the positive and pruning away the negative. It empowers us to become conscious architects of our own realities, weaving our dreams with intention and purpose.

The spectral circus, despite the receding echoes, persists. It is not an entity to be vanquished, but a reflection of the ever-shifting landscape of the subconscious. The unending show plays on, not as a source of fear and confusion, but as a constant reminder of the dynamic interplay between our inner and outer worlds. It is a call to continued exploration, a challenge to delve deeper into the mysteries of the self. The whispers in the willows may have quieted, but the wisdom they imparted continues to resonate within, guiding us towards a more complete and integrated existence. The journey beyond the veil is not a destination, but an ongoing process of becoming. It is a dance between the seen and unseen, a continuous exploration of the boundless universe that resides within each of us. And as we continue to explore, we learn to embrace the spectral circus within, recognizing it not as a haunting, but as a reflection of our own infinite potential. This ongoing process of discovery, fueled by the insights gained at Willowbrook, becomes a lifelong journey of self-realization. The whispers, once a source of fear, transform into a gentle guide, leading us ever deeper into the mysteries of our own being. The journey, ultimately, is one of returning home to ourselves.

7.1   A New Constellation

The whispers of Willowbrook had faded, the spectral calliope's haunting melody now a distant echo. The phantom clowns, their painted smiles finally revealing the silent tears beneath, had taken their final bow. The big top, once vibrant with ethereal light and the rustle of unseen wings, stood silent, its canvas tattered and bleached by the relentless sun. But the journey through its dreamlike landscapes had irrevocably altered the very fabric of my perception. I had navigated the labyrinth of my own subconscious, confronted the shadows lurking within, and learned to weave my own narrative within the dreamscape.

This journey through Willowbrook, a descent into the depths of the subconscious and an ascent into the celestial tapestry, had revealed a profound interconnectedness. The whispers of dead flora, deciphered through the Green Grimoire, resonated with the language of the stars. The celestial charts, once indecipherable, now mirrored the contours of my own mind, the astral plane a familiar pathway. The spectral circus, a macabre dance of forgotten memories and repressed emotions, had become a mirror reflecting the hidden landscapes within. And through this reflection, a profound transformation had begun.

The constellations themselves seemed to shift, rearrange, and coalesce into new formations. Stars I had known since childhood pulsed with a different light, their whispers carrying new meanings. It was as if the very act of mapping my inner world had caused a ripple effect throughout the cosmos, a celestial echo of the internal shifts I had experienced. This new celestial arrangement wasn't merely a visual phenomenon; it was a palpable shift in the energetic currents flowing through the universe. I felt it in the subtle vibrations of the earth beneath my feet, in the whispers of the wind through the now-silent willows, in the very air I breathed.

This new constellation, born from the echoes of Willowbrook's spectral circus, represented more than just a rearrangement of celestial bodies. It symbolized a re-ordering of my internal landscape, a restructuring of my understanding of the relationship between the conscious and subconscious mind. The rigid boundaries that once separated these realms had dissolved, replaced by a fluid, dynamic interplay. Dreams were no longer just fleeting phantoms of the night but vibrant portals into the hidden depths of my being, offering profound insights and guidance. I had learned to traverse the astral plane with confidence, navigating its ethereal currents with new-found understanding.

This newfound clarity extended beyond the realm of dreams and into my waking life. I perceived the world with heightened awareness, attuned to the subtle nuances of human interaction and the hidden currents of energy that flowed beneath the surface of everyday experience. The whispers of dead flora, once a cryptic language, now spoke to me of the interconnectedness of all living things, a testament to the cyclical nature of life, death, and rebirth. The celestial charts, once a representation of distant, unknowable forces, became a roadmap for navigating the inner cosmos, a guide to understanding the intricate dance between the self and the universe.

The transformation was not limited to my internal world. My interaction with the external world shifted as well. The veil between the seen and unseen had thinned, allowing me to glimpse the subtle energies that permeated every aspect of existence. I found myself drawn to places of power, ancient sites where the whispers of the past resonated with the present. I felt a deep connection to the natural world, a sense of kinship with the trees, the rivers, and the creatures of the forest. The world had become a living, breathing entity, pulsing with unseen energies and hidden meanings. This new constellation, this celestial re-alignment, was a testament to the transformative power of confronting the shadows of the subconscious. The journey through Willowbrook's spectral circus had been a harrowing one, a descent into the darkest recesses of my mind. But it had also been a journey of profound self-discovery, a pilgrimage to the heart of my own being. And from the ashes of this inner confrontation, a new sense of self had emerged, stronger, wiser, and more deeply connected to the universe. This wasn't just a new beginning, it was a rebirth.

This profound shift also instilled a deeper appreciation for the delicate balance between the seen and unseen, the conscious and subconscious, the earthly and the ethereal. The lessons learned within the spectral big top, amidst the haunting melodies and the silent tears of the clowns, had resonated far beyond the confines of Willowbrook Estate. They had seeped into the very core of my being, reshaping my perception of reality and my place within the grand cosmic tapestry. I had become a living embodiment of the interconnectedness of all things, a testament to the transformative power of the journey inward. The whispers of Willowbrook had faded, but their echoes would continue to reverberate throughout my life, shaping my path and guiding me towards a deeper understanding of the mysteries that lie beyond the veil. The show, in a sense, was far from over. It had simply transformed, evolving into a new and more profound expression of the unending dance between the conscious and the subconscious, the earthly and the divine. The journey continued, under the watchful gaze of the new constellation, a beacon in the ever-evolving landscape of my soul.

7.2 Seeds of Rebirth

The lingering scent of decaying flora, the phantom calliope's final, wheezing sigh, the fading laughter of spectral clowns – these are the remnants of the journey through Willowbrook's ethereal circus. We have delved into the cartography of the cosmos, navigated the astral plane, and deciphered the language of stars. We've spoken with the dead flora, learned the whispers of forgotten rituals from the Green Grimoire, and confronted the shadows of our own subconscious in the labyrinth of sleep. But what remains after the show's final curtain? What blossoms from the seeds sown in the fertile ground of the subconscious, tilled by the spectral plow of dream and nightmare?

The experience of Willowbrook is not simply a spectacle to be observed; it's a crucible for transformation. The echoes of laughter and loss, the haunting melodies, the poignant silent tears of the clowns—they are not mere phantoms of the past but catalysts for future growth. They are the raw materials from which we forge a new understanding of ourselves, our dreams, and the intricate tapestry that connects our inner world to the vast expanse of the cosmos. This understanding is not merely intellectual; it is visceral, etched into the very fabric of our being. It resonates within us, a subtle hum beneath the surface of waking life, reminding us of the hidden depths we carry within.

Consider the seeds of specific plants – the hardy dandelion, scattering its progeny on the wind, the tenacious burdock clinging to fur and fabric, the unassuming poppy spreading its vibrant bloom from the most unlikely of cracks in the pavement. Each possesses a unique strategy for survival and propagation, reflecting the resilience of life itself. Similarly, the insights gleaned from exploring Willowbrook's spectral circus take root within us, each finding its unique place within the landscape of our personal narrative. They may lie dormant for a time, awaiting the right conditions to germinate, but their potential remains. These seeds are not simply memories or intellectual concepts; they are imbued with the potent energy of the spectral realm, carrying the potential for profound personal growth.

This growth manifests in myriad ways. We might find ourselves more attuned to the subtle whispers of our intuition, more adept at navigating the complex emotional currents that flow beneath the surface of our daily lives. The once impenetrable labyrinth of sleep may begin to yield its secrets, revealing hidden pathways and unexpected vistas within the dreamscape. The spectral clowns, with their silent tears and painted smiles, offer a poignant reminder of the duality of human experience, the inextricable link between joy and sorrow, laughter and pain. Their presence echoes long after the circus has faded, prompting us to embrace the full spectrum of human emotion, to acknowledge the shadows as well as the light.

The process of integration is not always easy. It requires a willingness to confront uncomfortable truths, to delve into the hidden corners of our subconscious where fears and insecurities reside. It demands a courage born not of recklessness but of a deep and abiding faith in our own capacity for healing and transformation. This courage is not something we find outside ourselves; it is cultivated within, nurtured by the very experiences that challenge us to grow. Just as a gardener tends to the soil, preparing it for new life, so too must we cultivate the inner landscape of our being, creating fertile ground for the seeds of rebirth to take root.

Furthermore, this transformation extends beyond the individual. As we awaken to the interconnectedness of our inner and outer worlds, as we begin to decipher the language of the stars and comprehend the whispers of dead flora, we gain a deeper appreciation for the intricate web of life that connects us all. We recognize that our personal journey of self-discovery is interwoven with the collective evolution of consciousness, contributing to a larger narrative that unfolds across time and space. The spectral circus, with its cast of ethereal performers, becomes a microcosm of the human experience, reflecting our shared hopes, fears, and aspirations.

The seeds planted within us at Willowbrook bear the potential to blossom into a new understanding of ourselves and our place in the cosmos. They offer a path towards healing, integration, and a renewed sense of purpose. As we step beyond the veil of the spectral circus, we carry these seeds with us, scattering them like dandelion spores on the wind, planting them in the fertile ground of our everyday lives, watching as they take root and flourish, transforming the very landscape of our being. The show may be over, but the transformation has just begun. The cycle of death and rebirth continues, echoing the eternal dance of the cosmos, a dance in which we all play a part.

7.3 The Unending Show

The spectral circus isn't a performance with a defined beginning and end. It's a perpetual cycle, a carousel of archetypes and anxieties projected onto the decaying tapestry of Willowbrook. Think of it as an echo resonating through the dilapidated halls of the estate, each reverberation warping and distorting the original sound, adding layers of complexity and meaning. This isn't a show you can simply watch; it's one you participate in, whether you're aware of it or not. The whispers, the phantom calliope, the clowns' silent tears \item these aren't just isolated phenomena. They are interwoven threads in a larger, cosmic narrative, a narrative spun from the very fabric of your subconscious mind.

The ceaseless nature of this dream-woven circus is mirrored in the cyclical patterns of nature itself. Consider the seasons, the waxing and waning of the moon, the endless dance of life and death. These rhythms find their counterpart in the subconscious, where old traumas, buried desires, and forgotten memories resurface and play out in the theater of our dreams. The spectral circus embodies this eternal recurrence, a constant reminder that the past is never truly gone. It lingers, it whispers, it finds expression in the symbolic language of dreams, in the eerie laughter echoing through Willowbrook's empty rooms. This isn't about closure or resolution. This is about understanding the cyclical nature of the human experience and learning to navigate the ever-shifting landscapes of the inner world.

Just as the constellations wheel across the night sky, so too do the figures of the spectral circus dance across the stage of our subconscious. The Ringmaster, a shadowy figure embodying control and manipulation, might represent the ego's attempt to impose order on the chaotic realm of dreams. The trapeze artists, defying gravity with their graceful movements, might symbolize the precarious balance between conscious and unconscious desires. Each act, each character, holds a unique significance, offering a glimpse into the hidden depths of our psyche. These figures are not external entities, but projections of our own inner landscape. They are messengers from the subconscious, whispering secrets we may not be ready to hear, yet truths we cannot afford to ignore.

To understand the unending show is to accept that the exploration of the subconscious is a lifelong journey. There's no final curtain, no standing ovation, no encore. It's a continuous process of uncovering, interpreting, and integrating the fragmented narratives that make up our inner world. Imagine walking through a hall of mirrors, each reflection offering a distorted, yet revealing glimpse of yourself. That's the nature of this spectral circus. It challenges you to confront the multifaceted nature of your own being, to embrace the shadows alongside the light. And just as the cosmos are in constant flux, so too is the landscape of our subconscious, always shifting, always evolving.

This continuous unfolding is where the true power lies. By acknowledging the cyclical nature of the subconscious and the ever-present whispers of the spectral circus, we open ourselves to a deeper understanding of who we are. We gain access to a wellspring of creativity, intuition, and self-awareness. It's in the recognition of this endless performance that we find the potential for personal growth and transformation. The spectral circus isn't a haunting to be feared, but a guide to be embraced. It's a mirror reflecting the infinite possibilities within us, a constant reminder that the journey of self-discovery is a never-ending show. So, step right up, and embrace the whispers. The circus awaits.

Understanding this concept of the unending show allows us to engage with the subconscious in a more dynamic way. It's not about conquering or silencing the spectral circus, but about learning to dance with its rhythms. Just as the gardener tends to the cyclical growth and decay of the garden, so too must we tend to the ever-shifting landscapes of our inner world. This requires a willingness to embrace the unknown, to confront the shadows, and to accept the paradoxical nature of our dreams. It's a journey of continuous exploration, where each encounter with the spectral circus reveals a new facet of ourselves.

The unending nature of this inner spectacle also highlights the interconnectedness of all things. The spectral circus at Willowbrook isn't an isolated phenomenon. It's a microcosm of the larger cosmic drama, a reflection of the eternal dance of creation and destruction, order and chaos. Just as the stars influence the tides, so too do the archetypes of the subconscious shape our thoughts, emotions, and actions. By understanding this connection, we gain a deeper appreciation for the intricate web of existence and our place within it.

The cyclical nature of the show is not a limitation, but an invitation to continuous growth and transformation. Just as the seasons bring renewal and change, so too does the ongoing dialogue with our subconscious offer opportunities for healing and integration. It's a process of continual refinement, of shedding old patterns and embracing new possibilities. The unending show is not a prison, but a playground. It's a space where we can experiment, explore, and discover the hidden depths of our being.

Embracing the unending show means accepting the inherent ambiguity of the subconscious. There are no easy answers, no clear-cut interpretations. The spectral circus thrives on symbolism, metaphor, and paradox. It speaks in a language that requires patience, intuition, and a willingness to embrace the unknown. It's a journey of discovery, not a destination. And just as the cosmos continue to expand and evolve, so too does the landscape of our subconscious, offering endless opportunities for growth and exploration.

www.ingramcontent.com/pod-product-compliance
Ingram Content Group UK Ltd.
Pitfield, Milton Keynes, MK11 3LW, UK
UKHW021437240125

4283UKWH00041B/643

9 798348 371715